"I'm losing my mind!" I whispered. But not even insanity could explain how I had dreamed, or imagined, three names that I had later discovered on a gravestone in this churchyard. Stranger still, they were the children of the people who had once owned our land. . . .

I looked around wildly. Chad was gone. Or had he been here at all? Was he, too, a figment of my twisted imaginings? Was I here in this country graveyard with its narrow white church, or was it all something conjured up by my suddenly erratic mind . . . ?

I don't know how I got back to the house. When I looked out later, Annabel was parked in her usual place in the driveway, but I actually had no memory of having driven home.

In the Shadow of the White Rose

WANDA LUTTRELL

LIVING BOOKS
Tyndale House Publishers, Inc.
Wheaton, Illinois

First printing, July 1986
Library of Congress Catalog Card Number 86-50170
ISBN 0-8423-1602-7
Copyright © 1986 by Wanda Luttrell
Printed in the United States of America

For Johnny —
who "through the good or lean years"
has made it all worthwhile

ONE

At first, Tom said it was the lovely little valley and my own inner longings that had spoken to me so that day, that had made me see the house as I'd wanted to see it. But I knew better. I'd seen that house as plainly as I'd seen the woods and meadow around it, and it had reached out to me as no house ever had.

For some time I had wanted an old farmhouse like this one, as old as time, with restless memories and scarred woodwork and floors that showed evidence of those who had lived here. The weathered silver-gray wood of this house, with its steep-sloping roof and wide overhanging eaves, was exactly what I had in mind.

I stopped my '57 Chevy—affectionately called Annabel—in the middle of the road and sat absorbing the scene—the sunlight glinting on the small windowpanes, the dusty smell of summer intermingled with that of roses and mock orange, the whispering water in the creek, the drone of bees and wasps, and the chirping of crickets. From that first moment, I knew the place was mine. It belonged to me as surely as if I'd grown up there, a member of a loving family who had left it to me as my rightful heritage.

Perhaps it was my love of the place, a certain oneness I felt with it, that precipitated the whole nightmare. But that hot May afternoon as I crossed the little iron bridge and saw the house for the first time, I simply felt that safe, warm feeling of coming home.

I turned Annabel into the rutted, weed-covered lane that led around the edge of the meadow to the house. Not sure of the road, I parked there and got out.

The house beckoned to me as if it had been waiting patiently for me all through the years. Hot tears of happiness stung my eyes. I blinked them away, laughing at my foolishness. I'd never seen this place before in my life, and yet I was behaving like the prodigal child come home. Ridiculous as it might seem, though, I believed that no one who had grown up beneath those sheltering eaves could have felt any more welcome. I had no doubts whatsoever that I was home at last.

Suddenly the thought came to me that the place did not legally belong to me. I felt panicky. I *had* to have it! I had to find the legal owners and buy it. If it wasn't for sale, then I'd just have to convince them to sell it to me.

Surely it was empty. I could see no curtains at the dusty windows, no sign of anything but wildlife. A white rosebush spread its thorny canes beneath the front window, scenting the drowsy afternoon with its creamy white blossoms. Even from where I stood halfway up the lane, I could smell the heady perfume that is exclusively rose. I could hear the buzzing of bees as they gathered its sweet nectar.

Suppressing my longing to go to the house, I turned and ran back to Annabel. I could hardly wait to bring Tom here. *Perhaps he already knows the place,* I thought. He had lived on the other side of the nearby town until he was eighteen years old. Surely he would love the place as I did! He would have room here for the hunting dogs he wanted, and, best of all, there would be room for children—three or four at least, boys and girls; it didn't matter. Maybe we would adopt some of them. And how they'd love that creek and the big woods and meadow!

I thought with pleasure of leaving the cramped city apartment where Tom and I had lived for the past three years. Here we could have real flower beds and a vegetable garden. We would move just as soon as we could get a deed drawn up and do whatever repairing was absolutely necessary. I didn't even care if there was plumbing in the house right now. Modern convenience could be had for a price; this feeling I had could not be bought for any amount of money.

Looking back at the house one last time, I noted that the sun was traveling down the sky behind the house. That meant it faced east and the sunrise. I hoped the window over the white rosebush opened into a bedroom. One large room apparently extended from the front of the house to the back, because through a back window I could see the lacy branches of locust trees. As a matter of fact, it seemed I could see an unbroken line of trees right through the whole house! I shut my eyes, then looked again. It must be the shimmering heat waves between me and the house that made those wavery lines which looked like trees, I decided.

I returned to thoughts of that big bedroom behind the white rosebush. With the window open, that heady scent would permeate the whole room, and each morning we would be awakened by the gentle fingers of the first morning light reaching in our window, playing over the patchwork quilt on the big old walnut bed. . . .

I had to laugh at myself again. I didn't even own a patchwork quilt, much less the high old walnut bed I'd envisioned so plainly. But it was a patchwork-and-antique kind of house. *That's why my vision of the bedroom was so vivid,* I thought. Vivid, down to the yellow wheat-sprigged border around the top of the soft gray-blue walls and the braided rug on the wide planks of golden wood that formed the polished floor.

The sky darkened from a cloud passing across the sun, and I was reminded that the day was slipping away. I got in the car, started it up, then backed out onto the narrow blacktop road and headed back the way I had come. If there was time, I'd inquire about this apparently abandoned place at the courthouse in the county seat a few miles away. I was sorry now I'd wasted the morning wandering along all those lovely country lanes searching, as I'd searched for over a year now, for a place we could call home.

Tom was wanting to set up a law practice of his own, possibly here in his old hometown where his grandfather had practiced law years ago. I didn't care where we lived. I had no hometown ties. I simply wanted a home of our own somewhere. Apartment living just wasn't for me. I wanted an ancestral home and memories I could adopt and substitute for those of my own childhood years, spent in a series of foster homes and an orphanage boarding school where I'd finished high school.

Some people are happy to be always on the move—their hearts know what the wild goose knows. My father was one of those. My mother followed wherever he led until she died in childbirth in the primitive wilds of Alaska. The baby died, too, and I was left alone at the age of three with my father. He immediately placed me in a foster home. If either my father or my mother had any living relatives, I never knew them.

Since my father never actually gave me up for adoption by some stable family, I was passed around from one foster home to another like an unwanted kitten. Wherever I lived during those years, I had learned to be fairly content by growing a hard, protective shell that allowed no one to get close enough to hurt me and by refusing to put down any roots that might be yanked up just when they had begun to thrive. After meeting and marrying Tom, I could feel the roots I'd kept dormant all those years reaching out for some settled place where they could sink deep into welcoming soil. Now I could feel them pulling me back to the house.

I shook myself mentally and forced myself to concentrate on driving. I didn't even remember recrossing the little iron bridge, and here I was almost back in town.

High cliffs rose up on one side of the road, and the ground sheered off on the other side down to the river. These natural barriers had kept the town from spreading in this direction, although it didn't appear to have spread much anyway. There were the usual small suburbs with several streets of copycat houses surrounding the town. The downtown area consisted of four streets of small, neat shops built in a square around a pre-Civil War Greek Revival courthouse, its graceful white columns and dignified cupola set back amid fine old trees.

A sign forbade traffic in the square, where a half-dozen old men sat idly on stone benches scattered around the flower beds. Green antique lampposts dripped white globes like giant tears. Another dozen or so men in short-sleeved shirts and women in sleeveless dresses stared at me, ignored me, or smiled and spoke amiably as I left the car on the perimeter of the square and made my way up the brick walk to the courthouse. The path split at a war-dead memorial and rejoined on the other side to reach the courthouse steps.

It seems like a fairly friendly little town, I thought, as I pushed through the heavy doors and left the bright May afternoon for the comparative gloom of old stone. My footsteps echoed hollow on the marble floor of the hall.

A County Court Clerk sign stuck out about halfway down the hall. As I entered the office, one of the busy clerks looked up with a "May I help you?"

"The abandoned place about five miles down Deserted Creek Road—I think that's the name—do you know if it's for sale?" I asked eagerly.

The young clerk wrinkled her smooth forehead with a frown, laid her cigarette across an ashtray, and tossed her long brown hair over her shoulder. "I'm not familiar with that road at all, ma'am," she said finally, making my twenty-four years seem like fifty. "I'll call Mr. Roberts. He's been county clerk forever. He knows every plot of ground in the county!"

She smiled at me, then turned to the back of the room hidden from my view by an ell. From floor to ceiling and running out of my sight around the ell were shelves of huge leather-bound volumes, deed books and so forth, I guessed. "Mr. Roberts?" the young woman called. "Can you come up front?"

"Be right there!" a deep masculine voice answered. *If Mr. Roberts is as attractive as his voice,* I thought, *no wonder this clerk's checking her false eyelashes and makeup.* She'd whipped out a compact mirror from under the counter and replaced it in a moment's time.

I couldn't have been more surprised to see the owner of that intriguing voice. He was tall, thin almost to emaciation, white-haired, and at least seventy years old. As he paced toward me, Mr. Roberts' intense gaze missed nothing that might help to catalog this stranger in their midst. I almost expected him to file me neatly away in one of the big leather volumes when he had finished.

"Is there something I can do for you, little lady?" he asked, leaning on the counter and looking at me intently out of penetrating gray eyes under thick bony brows.

"I hope so," I answered and described the sheltered little valley I'd found and asked if it was for sale.

"Deserter's Creek," he corrected, "not Deserted. Name goes clean back to the Civil War." I nodded impatiently. "Place by the creek, just past the bridge, you mean? Nice meadow surrounded by wooded hills. Four and three-quarter miles from this courthouse exactly. Yes, ma'am, I know it. The old Adams place. And it is for sale. Belongs to Jim Tupts now, works out to the distillery."

"Do you have any idea what he's asking for it?" My knees felt weak. Tom was a very junior partner in the law firm. I wanted the old man to name a price we could afford—property was so high now.

"No, I don't know what he's askin', Miz, ah . . . ?"

"Farris. Amanda Farris."

"New around here, ain't you?"

"We're from Fayette County." I felt impatient to get the credentials out of the way and get on with my inquiry, but Mr. Roberts wasn't ready yet.

"You're 'welcome as kindly showers to the long parched earth,' " he quoted. "Dryden. Any kin to old Judge Farris who used to be Chief Justice of the Court of Appeals up to Frankfort? Fine man, the judge. He was from here, you know. I thought a lot of him. His son got killed over in Korea, I recollect. Tom, Jr., that was. He left a widow and a young son. Miz Farris died when the boy was seventeen or eighteen years old, just out of high school. The grandparents are gone, too, now—"

"My husband is Tom Farris, III." I cut in before he could get started on all that. "Judge Farris was his grandfather. I never knew him." My impatience must have shown in my voice. The girl was staring at me open-mouthed.

"Well, well! Yep, the judge was a good friend of mine till the day he died," he went on. "Miz Farris." He rubbed one hand thoughtfully over a faint stubble of white beard on his hollow cheeks. "I'll ring ole Jim and see what he wants for that property, if it'll be any help to you."

"Oh, yes, if you would, please, Mr. Roberts!" I said. "I would appreciate it very much!"

"Janie, get me Jim Tupts out to the distillery, will you, honey?" he said, turning to the clerk who put the call through and handed the phone to him.

"Jim? Rob, here. How ya been, you ole horse thief? Ain't seen you around in a coon's age!" He listened, then chuckled once or twice between "Humphs."

"You mean, you're married to Tom Farris?" Janie asked. I nodded. "Wow! I'll never forget that state tournament when Tom Farris dropped in the last basket just as the whistle blew and we won by two points! I was just a kid, but I'll never forget it! He made all-tournament team and went on to play at UK. Tom Farris! Wow!"

It was my first encounter with Tom's hometown fans. I smiled at her warmly and turned my attention back to what Mr. Roberts was saying into the phone.

"What I called you about, Jim, is the ole Deserter's Creek place. You still wanta sell? Well, I figured that. Listen, there's a little lady here askin' 'bout it. Little Tom Farris' wife." *(Little Tom is over six feet tall,* I told him silently.) "What're you askin' now?" Mr. Roberts laughed appreciatively. "OK, Jim. I'll take care of it. Yeah, glad to oblige. I'll let you know." He hung up.

I had fingers on both hands crossed, but he named

a figure that seemed ridiculously low to me. I must
have looked shocked.

"Says he won't take a cent less!" he said firmly.

"But, Mr. Roberts, even if the house is in bad repair,
and it doesn't seem to be in such bad shape, isn't
that awfully low?" I was too surprised to bargain
sensibly. "Not that I'm arguing with the price! It
sounds great. . . . Of course, I'll have to talk it over
with my husband, first. But—"

"Miz Farris," he interrupted, "did I understand you
to say, 'the house'?"

"Yes, of course. There may be damage inside, and
for all I know, the roof may leak. I didn't go all the
way up the lane. But the walls and chimney look
sound, and I didn't see a single missing windowpane.
That in itself is remark—"

"Miz Farris," Mr. Roberts interrupted again, his
keen eyes studying me closely, "there ain't no house
on Jim Tupts' property on Deserter's Creek."

"But of course there's a house! That's why I want
it so badly—that silvery weathered wood and those
wide overhanging eaves and the small, old-fashioned
panes in the windows. Why, there's even a white rose
blooming under the window. You must be thinking
of some other piece of land. . . ."

Mr. Roberts was staring at me, his eyes narrowed,
all traces of old-fashioned gallantry and banter replaced with some kind of fierce conviction.

"There *was* a house like that on the old Adams
place, Miz Farris," he said finally, his silken voice
whispery now. "It's been gone for over fifty years,
burned to the ground long before you was born!"

"How dare you ridicule me, just because I'm new in these parts! Of course there's a house. I saw it with my own eyes." I turned and left, slamming his door behind me.

T W O

"That pompous old yokel poking fun at the stranger in town!" I stormed, pacing the floor in Tom's small office. "And he didn't even crack a smile!"

"Sit down, sweetheart, before you wear a path in the carpet!" Tom ordered.

"But it was such a tasteless joke!" I sputtered. Then once more I recalled the serious, wide-eyed look on Janie's face and Mr. Roberts' look of genuine puzzlement as I'd stalked out of the county court clerk's office. *Could I have misjudged the old man?* I wondered for the hundredth time since I'd headed Annabel back toward Lexington. *But I saw that house!*

"I remember old Mr. Rob," Tom said. "He and Granddad were cronies. Amanda, country towns are . . . well, they can be vicious. Some of them eat newcomers for breakfast. Old Rob, though, just has a weird sense of humor."

"You can say that again!"

"Old Rob just has a wei—"

"Oh, all right, you big dope!" I laughed, leaning down to place a kiss on the sun crinkles that appeared at the corners of his blue eyes as he laughed up at me.

He pulled me down onto his lap. "That's better!" he said, fitting me into the curve of his arms like a familiar piece of an often-worked jigsaw puzzle. His kiss was slow, deliberate, and very thorough. I snuggled against him, loving the way my head fit the hollow of his shoulder, the protective feel of his strong arms around me. But Tom picked me up, carried me across the room, and deposited me in a brown leather chair.

"Now stay there and be quiet till I get this brief finished and we'll go take a look at this house of yours. It'll be daylight for several hours, thanks to daylight saving time and—"

"You mean we'll go back today?" I interrupted eagerly.

He nodded. "I might as well get it over with. I can see I'll get no peace until I visit this ancestral home of yours."

I ignored his sarcasm. "Do you know the place I'm talking about, Tom?"

He shook his head. "I know Deserter's Creek Road fairly well. It used to be the local lovers' lane. But I don't recall a house like you described. Still, it's been a long time. . . ."

I pushed aside the stab of jealousy his admitted knowledge of lovers' lane aroused. "You'll adore this place!" I insisted. "It's perfect for us! And you can have those dogs you've been wanting. It's perfect for children, too. And I'll bet there's not a decent lawyer in the whole county! You could set up that practice you've been talking about—"

"Whoa, sweetheart!" he interrupted. "I grew up in that particular town. That's why I asked you to scout around down that way. But you might not like it there, being a big city gal and all. I'll admit I'd like the intimacy of a small-town practice like my grand-dad had there. That was before he was made a judge, when I was just a kid. But I still remember that office and the people who came and went, all of them special friends of his, or so it seemed. I'd have contacts there because of him. It just might work out. Corporate law pays well, eventually, but it's too impersonal. I like working with people."

"I know!" I groaned, and he had the grace to laugh. We both knew he was inclined to bring stray people home with him the way some kids carry stray animals home. People from all sectors of society had paraded in and out of our small apartment near Tom's office. The only requirement was that they have some prob-lem or trouble with which he could help. Sometimes he just wanted to "introduce them to my best Friend," as he put it. I had fixed countless meals and beds on the couch for down-and-outers being rehabilitated, or "led to the Lord," by my loving husband.

How could I complain, though? Hadn't I been one of his earlier projects—the poor little half-orphan who needed love? And he had turned out to be so right for me. I hadn't even known how desperately I needed love until Tom came along.

I sat quietly waiting for him to finish his work, remembering those first frightening days when I had come straight from high school to work in the big law firm as a steno in the stenographic pool. One day I had been chosen to fill in for an older steno who was ill and I had begun taking dictation from one of the firm's junior partners—Tom Farris.

The girls had oohed and aahed at that, and one of them had warned, "Play it cool, Amanda! He's a capital *E,* capital *B!*"—"Eligible Bachelor," the most important topic of conversation in the steno pool. I had laughed and gone innocently off to Mr. Farris' office—only to have my lonely life completely transformed.

Of course, it didn't happen in that one afternoon, but I did more and more of his work. Then he began to take me out. First a lunch here, a dinner there, then movies, plays, concerts, ball games. The girls were openly envious, partly because I hadn't tried to win Tom's attention in any of their usual, obvious ways.

Now after three years as Tom's wife, I was convinced that it had been my lonely little orphan status that had intrigued him. Back then, though happy about his attraction to me, I didn't pretend to understand it. Neither had the other girls.

"What's with those cold green eyes and that tipped-up nose to snag Tom Farris?" Betty Jo asked the day that was to be my last in the steno pool before our marriage. I was back in the supply room, but I could hear every word.

"Beats me," another girl—*Emily,* I thought—had answered. "But I think we're just having a bad case of sour grapes! And you have to admit she's cute, and all that thick, dark hair—"

"Well, anyway," a voice I couldn't identify cut in,

"Tom Farris ain't Robert Redford, you know! He must be past thirty!"

"Oh, but, honey, he's all man!" That was Betty Jo again. "And those sultry blue eyes and those white eyelashes send cold chills down my spine!"

Tom's eyelashes weren't white. I looked at them, shadowing his tanned cheeks as he concentrated on the papers on his desk. Like his hair, they were a very pale blond. But I knew what Betty Jo meant, though I still resented her for having said it.

Tom was a very attractive man—tall and hard-muscled with the deep, all-year-round tan of the outdoorsman. And the same sun and wind that had produced the tan had given him those adorable sun crinkles around the eyes and a dusting of freckles across the nose. Fifteen, to be exact. I knew and loved every one of them. To me, Tom was all the special feelings I hadn't known since my mother died, and much more.

The only things I actually remembered about my mother were the warm, safe feeling of her arms when she rocked me or when I crept into bed with her after a nightmare and the sweet, clean scent that always clung to her skin and hair. Those were the things I had longed for in the long, lonely nights when Mama was no longer there.

I had two things that had belonged to her—a worn black Bible and a wallet-sized black-and-white photograph showing a small, dark-haired woman standing on a long porch with her arms around a two- or three-year-old girl.

Sometimes, when I was feeling especially lonely

in a new foster home, or when a foster sibling or a new schoolmate let me know I really didn't belong, I'd thumb through Mama's Bible, lingering at the passages she had underlined, running my finger over the faded pencil marks, trying to recapture some small part of her.

She seemed to have liked the verses that told of Jesus. I could identify with him: "a man of sorrows," "despised and rejected," "acquainted with grief." But I didn't like God the Father very much. Some of my foster families had attended church and Sunday school, and some of them had sent their children and me to Vacation Bible School and church camp where we studied about God the Father and Jesus, his Son, and the Holy Spirit. I didn't understand the Spirit. I felt sorry for Jesus and a little superior to him because *I* was tough enough to survive in this old world. I equated God, who had turned his back on Jesus as he died on the cross, with my own father, who had turned his back on me.

For a long time, I had dreams of my father coming for me. "I'm taking you with me, Mandy," he would say. (I didn't like that nickname and had fought many a battle over it at school, but it was sort of special to allow him alone to use it.) In my dream I would ride off with him into the sunset to live happily ever after.

He actually visited me half a dozen times after Mama died. When he came, he would take me somewhere for an hour or two, buy me ice cream or some other treat, and ask the same old perfunctory questions. I was twelve years old before I realized he couldn't have cared less about the answers, no matter how fiercely I pretended otherwise, and I determined that no one, not even God, would ever get close enough to hurt or reject me again.

Then into my narrow life had come Tom. It was like opening up a small, stuffy room and letting in fresh air and sunlight. With Elizabeth Barrett Browning, I loved him with "the height and breadth and depth my soul can feel when feeling out of sight." To hear him call me "sweetheart" in that special way of his or to see that very special look of love in his eyes just for me made up for all "my lost saints" or those I'd never had.

If anyone had told me, that day in Tom's office, that anything could come between us, I would have laughed in his face. What we had was too good to ruin, and I had no intention of losing him. That day I was too comfortably wrapped in Tom's love to have any fears for our future. *Nothing matters to me now but Tom and our love,* I thought as I watched him gather up his papers and put them into his briefcase.

And the house. The thought came full-blown and totally unexpected, but I could feel its strange power reaching across the miles, pulling me to it. . . .

Surely Tom will love it as I do! I thought. My old love and my new must love each other. *But what if he doesn't?* Of course, I couldn't give up Tom for the house. That was ridiculous. But could I give up my newfound home for Tom? I knew I should have been able to answer that without hesitation, with an emphatic *yes!* Somehow I wasn't sure I could.

"Ready, Manda?" Tom asked, and I jumped up, feeling guilty at my thoughts, eager to get started back to my house.

Soon we were passing the little white church on the left, the last building before our house. (Already I had begun thinking of it as ours.)

"It's right across this next little bridge, Tom," I said. "The lane's rough, just ruts and weeds. I wouldn't take Annabel up there. And since this Chrysler is second only to me in your life, or have I got that backwards . . . ?" I teased.

Tom was frowning, as though he knew where he was and yet wasn't sure.

"Park just inside the lane, off the road, and we can walk up to the house," I suggested. "Oh, look at the sunlight on the cliffs above the creek! It wasn't like that—"

"Amanda," Tom broke in, "are you sure this is the place?" His voice sounded strange, and I turned to look at him.

"Of course, I'm sure! I could find it blindfolded! See? Just up on that. . . ." I let the words trail away.

Across the weed-grown meadow framed by the woods, tall sedge and locust sprouts waved in the slight evening breeze. There was nothing else on the rise—no gray house, nothing at all.

THREE

My eyes searched the little valley frantically. There was no sign of a weathered gray house. In fact, there was no house of any kind anywhere in sight.

"I don't understand," I whispered. "Tom, don't look at me like that! I saw that house! It was right here!"

Tom laughed a little uncertainly. Then he began backing the car out onto the paved road. "Honey, you must be mistaken in the location. That would explain the mix-up between you and Mr. Rob at the courthouse today, too. The old man must have been thinking of this place, very similar to the one you meant. I remember passing this place on fishing and swimming trips. There never was a house here that I can remember. We'll just drive a little farther down the road and find your gray house."

I nodded in agreement, but I wasn't convinced. The bridge across the creek, the meadow, the woods— all were exactly as I remembered them, except that the house was gone.

The road and the creek ran into the river a mile or so past the bridge. There were no more houses on that road at all and no other bridges. Even between here and town, that was the only bridge.

Tom pulled back into the lane. He hadn't looked directly at me for several minutes now.

The rise was bathed in a golden glow of sunset that turned the green leaves of the trees and the grass of the meadow to a pale green-gold. I still loved the little valley in its sheltering circle of hills and trees, still felt at home in it, house or no house.

But what could it mean? Had I seen a mirage in the afternoon? I didn't know if mirages happened anywhere outside the desert or not, but I had seen pools of water on the highway which, when I drove through them, weren't there at all. Perhaps something similar had happened here today. It had been much more than a pool of water caused by shimmering heat waves, though. I had seen every detail of that house even down to the small windowpanes and the white rosebush.

"Tom, look!" I shouted. "It's there!"

He threw me a quick glance, then turned to look at the rise. The look of horror on his face when he turned back to me was almost comical.

"Now see here, Amanda," he said firmly, "there's no house on that—"

"No, no. The rose! The white rose is there! It's blooming just as it was this afternoon. I didn't imagine that, at least!" Then I had a frightening thought. "Tom? You *do* see the rosebush, don't you?" I let my breath out in a long sigh of relief at his nod.

"Yes, I see the bush. It's full of white roses." He

took the keys out of the ignition and sat fiddling with them, a frown creasing his forehead. If I hadn't known Tom so well, I'd have thought he was worried, but Tom never worried. He based his life on Proverbs chapter 3, verses 5 and 6: "Trust in the Lord with all thine heart; and lean not unto thine own understanding. In all thy ways acknowledge him, and he shall direct thy paths."

"With God on your side, how can you lose?" I'd heard him tell the strays he brought home. I often wondered if Tom had missed his calling, if he should have been a minister or a social worker. Except that he would have had to preach with his bags packed ready to move on, because he didn't know how to avoid controversy. And social workers aren't supposed to get personally involved. Tom could never stay impersonal.

"Amanda," he began hesitantly, "do you see anything else on the rise now?" His eyes held a troubled look I didn't remember ever seeing in them before.

"No, Tom, of course not. Not now. The broom sedge and locust sprouts are all growing where the house stood. But I saw that house this afternoon as plain as we can see the rosebush now. If you'd been with me, I know you'd have seen it, too! There was one strange thing, though. I thought I saw an unbroken line of trees through the house. Tom, could it have been some kind of mirage? A very vivid one?"

The cloud that had come over his eyes cleared some. "It must have been something like that, Amanda. Or some interplay of sun and shadow seen through heat waves in the meadow."

Somehow, I still couldn't quite accept his explanation, but there seemed to be no other. All I was sure of was that I'd seen the house in the afternoon and now it was gone. I was greatly disappointed. How I had wanted that old house!

All at once I knew what to do. "Tom, let's buy the place anyway," I suggested eagerly. "We could build a house here to suit ourselves—something all wood and stone to blend in with the natural setting. It's a beautiful little valley, and already it seems like home to me."

Tom studied me seriously for several seconds. "Sweetheart, if you're sure it's what you want, we'll buy it. I've enough money to buy the land at the price Mr. Rob quoted you, with enough left over to set up a small office if I decide to hang out my own shingle. We can get a loan when we're ready to build the house."

"Oh, Tom, let's do it now! Let's start building right away and try to move in before Christmas. It would be so lovely to spend Christmas in our own home. Do you realize that's something I've never done in my whole life as long as I can remember?" I was playing on his overabundant sympathy, but it was true, and I'd use any help I could get in obtaining this place. I felt compelled to own it.

He reached over and ruffled my hair. "OK, sweetheart. I know how badly you want a home, and I can't blame you. We'll do it, just as soon as I can get a clear deed to the place and a loan. House payments probably won't run much more than the rent we're throwing away on our apartment in Lexington." He smiled at me with so much love in his blue eyes that I felt tears sting my own.

"You decide what kind of house you want, and I'll scout around for a builder. Some local fellow would be best, I think. Cheaper and more convenient. . . ." He frowned. "I've lost touch with local people. Maybe Mr. Rob could recommend someone. Why don't you ask him?" he suggested with a sly grin.

"Oh, Tom, I couldn't! He must think I'm insane anyway after this afternoon. I don't think I could face him!"

Tom just sat there looking at me with that half smile on his lips. I could feel a flush mounting my face.

"I get the message," I said finally. "I owe him an apology for today. All right, St. Thomas, I'll do it, but I don't have to like it!"

He laughed. "One of these days that temper will get you in more than merely an embarrassing situation, sweetheart," he warned as he started the Chrysler and backed onto the road. "And the old man isn't—what did you call him?—a frustrated tragedian. He was right all along. I'd love to see this touching little scene of apology. I think I'll take tomorrow off and go with you."

I made a face at him. "If you do, I won't go. And if you don't stop that idiotic laughing and watch the road, I'm going to drive!"

The threat sobered him instantly. His small confidence in my driving ability had prompted him to buy me Annabel right after I'd received my license. But his little joke had backfired. I had grown so attached to Annabel that he couldn't get me to part with her when her shabbiness had begun to embarrass him.

"Let's trade that wreck in for something at least

made in the eighties," he'd begged not long ago. "It's beginning to spoil my image as a successful young lawyer."

"That's Annabel you're talking about, Tom Farris!" I had protested. "And she's not about to be traded in where some hot-rod-happy kid can get his hands on her! She's mine and I aim to keep her and you might just as well learn to live with her!"

He had groaned in mock despair. Or had it been real? "That's what I get for putting the bill of sale in your name. I'm helpless!"

I had let him "persuade" me to have her painted, reupholstered, and tuned up, but Annabel stayed.

My strong feelings of attachment to my possessions, I supposed, were an overreaction to my having moved from pillar to post all my life. Whenever I bought something, I bought it for keeps. Even though I'd known from the first that Tom was the one I wanted, marrying him had not been a hasty, impulsive thing. I had dated him for two years before finally agreeing to marriage, for I knew that once we were married, it would be for the rest of our lives.

For me, buying a home would be like marriage, or so I thought. If we moved to this valley along Deserter's Creek, I would never move again. Still, in spite of my unusually quick decision about buying the place, I had no doubts whatever. I felt nothing but happiness at the thought that this would be my home for the rest of my life.

For the next few days, I pored over plan books. I drove all over Lexington looking at houses—ranch styles, split levels, Southern colonials, pseudo-colonials. None of them seemed right for our ten acres on Deserter's Creek. I nearly drove Tom crazy, for every time we thought we had found a halfway suitable plan, I had an absurd desire to cry. None of them satisfied me.

"I don't know, Amanda," Tom said at last, "maybe we'd better wait until you know what you want." There was a justifiable edge to his voice.

Suddenly I knew why none of the plans pleased me. None of them fit the picture in the back of my mind of a weathered gray house with a steep roof and wide overhanging eaves. I stopped my pacing midway across the living room.

"Tom, I know exactly the house I want, but I'm pretty sure it won't be in any of the plan books. Couldn't we draw our own plans?"

"Sweetheart, the only thing I can draw is conclusions," he said with a laugh. "I couldn't draw a straight line with a ruler. An architect should be able to draw plans from a sketch and a description, though, if you're that sure of what you want."

In reply, I picked up all the plan books and dumped them in the trash basket. "Do you know any architects?" I perched on the arm of his easy chair.

"Let's see. There was a fellow, Bryan somebody, I went to school with at UK. Can't remember his last name, though."

Already I was thumbing through the Yellow Pages of the phone book. "Here's a list, but Tom, there's scads of them!"

"Try to pick one just starting out on his own, not one of the large firms. He'll be more likely to want a small job like this and may be cheaper."

I smiled at him fondly. He was showing empathy

for someone whose boat he was likely to share in the near future, if his plans for his own office worked out.

I ran my finger down the list of architects, passing up the five- and six-name "associates," and stopped at the first loner I came to. Of course, he might be an old established firm, for all I knew.

" 'Eric Dunaway, Architect,' " I read aloud. " 'Member of American Institute of Architects.' How does that sound, Tom?"

"Fine," he mumbled from deep in some law book.

I left him there and went into the bedroom to use the phone. I reached Mr. Dunaway at home and set up an appointment for the next day.

He was younger than I had expected, with curly Orphan Annie hair and a firm belief in seeing the site before he tried to draw plans for it. I led the way in Annabel, and he followed in his red Corvette so he could go back to his office while I finished my business at the courthouse. I was pleased that I had chosen, at random, an architect who cared enough to drive all the way out to Deserter's Creek to "get the feel of the place," as he said.

He walked all around the rise where the house would stand, then stood on the rise looking out over the meadow.

"OK," he said finally, "I can see it now, just as it ought to look, Mrs. Farris. Wide eaves, narrow windowpanes, sort of a modified Cape Cod three-quarter house, no dormers, wide weatherboarding, an entrance hall, and spacious but cozy rooms."

A thrill of excitement traveled down my spine. "You actually see the house?" I asked eagerly. "That's not just a figure of speech?"

He laughed. "Well, I practically see it, but I guess it's more of a mental vision. Still, I've 'seen' enough to know how to draw your plans."

I sighed. I couldn't actually see the house today, either. I wasn't sure if I should be disappointed or relieved.

"You wouldn't happen to know a good local contractor, would you?" I asked as we went to our cars, still hoping to avoid another encounter with Mr. Roberts.

"Afraid not, Mrs. Farris," he answered. "I know several in Fayette County, but it would be prohibitively expensive to bring them up here. You'd better check with someone local on that."

Mr. Roberts, I thought resignedly. I stood watching as the little red car roared across the bridge and around the bend. Then, not wanting to leave the place, I closed Annabel's door and walked back up to the rise.

The air was heavy and warm, sustaining the drone of bees. The sky was that soft, deep blue of early summer, with buttermilk clouds spilled all across it. It would have been a perfect day for a picnic in the meadow or by the creek, but I hadn't thought to bring a lunch. It was early, though; lunch could wait. I would enjoy my valley while I had the chance.

I strolled around the meadow at the edge of the woods, breathing in the soft, unpolluted air of country summer, fragrant with wildflowers and lush green growth. Up near the rise, the white rose put all other pleasant scents to shame. Behind the rise, near the woods, I removed my shoes, yielding to the temptation of a large patch of incredibly fine green grass, perhaps a holdover from some long-lost lawn. It was tall now, as tall as bluegrass ever gets, and was forming its bluish purple bloom.

I sank back into the grass on my elbows, then rolled to my stomach and lay across the slope, dreamily trying to picture the people who had lived here, possibly in my elusive gray house. Had it been built in early pioneer days? It certainly had been more sophisticated than a rough pioneer cabin, but, then, many early Kentucky houses had been nothing short of mansions. Add another fifty or sixty years, though. Civil War times?

Behind me leaves rustled in the gentle breeze, and I could hear the gossipy whispering of the cedar branches in a tall, dark thicket halfway up the hill. I settled deeper into the bluegrass. I tried to visualize the gray house as I had seen it before, but although I could "see" it in memory, the actual clear-cut vision of a few days ago was not there. The white rosebush, though, stood below me as I had first seen it, the sun casting its shadow across the empty space where the house surely had stood.

I closed my eyes halfway and looked through a haze of eyelashes, as I had done as a child conjuring up fantasies, trying to picture a Civil War couple—she with hair piled on top of her head, probably wearing full, sweeping skirts, and he in a uniform of blue or gray. Would he have been a Rebel or a Yankee? It was hard to say, since Kentucky never had left the Union officially. For a time, though, the Commonwealth— birthplace of both Abe Lincoln and Jeff Davis—had both a Southern and a Northern government, and as many of her sons in gray as in blue. I couldn't decide which uniform my dark-eyed Deserter's Creek resident had worn. . . .

. . . *Children were down in the creek bed. I could hear them calling to each other as they played. I stood up slowly. A strange lethargy seemed to have overtaken me. Yes, I could see them now—brown-eyed Susannah in her blue gingham dress with long brown pigtails and the ends of her white petticoats tied up around her waist. Her long drawers showed white in the sunlight as she splashed across the shallow pool, staggering under the burden of a heavy rock she was carrying to her older brothers for the dam they were building.*

Harrison's green eyes smiled up at her as he took the rock and began fitting it into the dam. Black-eyed Tarrellton held one hand under the water, then flung it up suddenly, sending a huge-pinchered crawfish and a spray of water onto his sister.

Susannah screamed and staggered backward into the water. Harrison hit Tarrellton in a flying leap, and the boys thrashed at each other, spraying the water up in white geysers that fell in sun-sparkled drops around them. Susannah sat in the water, her eyes wide and tearful. Steady, serious Harrison, the eldest, always took Susannah's part, but I knew she loved wild, fierce Tarrellton best. It was just something she couldn't help, and, try as I would, neither could I.

Suddenly I became aware of a darkening of the sunlight around me. It was going to storm. I put my hands down to push up from the ground where I lay again without remembering lying down. Then the shadow shifted, and I looked up into Tarrellton's dark eyes. I knew I should scold him for being mischievous again, but his eyes stared back at me, insolent and unflinching. . . .

. . . "Tarrellton," I said. Then I sat upright. I didn't know anyone named Tarrellton! It was a name I'd never heard before. Had I fallen asleep and dreamed about the three children in the creek? They were gone now, had never been there, I supposed.

It must all have been a dream, I thought. But who was this dark-eyed boy of ten or eleven? A leftover from my dream? I closed my eyes tightly, then opened them. Dark eyes met mine in an intent, mutually curious stare.

"Who are you?" I whispered.

"Ain't no need to whisper, lady," he said. "Don't reckon there's a soul in a mile a here."

"Who are you?" I repeated louder this time. "Where did you come from?"

"Name's Chad Palmer. I live up the road apiece. Where'd *you* come from?" he asked.

He's as insolent as Tarrellton ever. . . . STOP IT! I ordered silently. That had been a dream! I wasn't so sure I was awake even now. My head hurt and I felt exhausted, for no reason that I knew.

"I'm from Lexington," I answered. "My husband and I have bought this place."

Chad grinned, showing even white teeth against swarthy skin that may have been dark as much from dirt as from suntan. His dark hair, a rough, sun-streaked thatch, hung over his ears and onto his neck. He wore faded blue jeans cut off above the knees, but no shirt or belt, and the jeans hung loosely from his scrawny, tanned body. His bare feet were indescribably dirty, scratched, and toughened. But his hands and nails, I noticed in surprise, were clean.

He caught my stare and stuffed his hands into his front pockets. "Been catchin' crawdads down in the creek," he muttered, as though feeling the need to apologize for clean hands. *Or is he just naturally sullen and belligerent?* I wondered.

"You gonna live here?" he asked, studying me seriously.

I nodded. "Yes, we're planning to build a house here."

The dark eyes never left mine, but they widened, then narrowed, his thoughts obscure but busy behind them. One filthy foot rubbed idly over the top of the other one. Then his lips curved in a mocking smile, much too old for his years. He shook his head slowly from side to side.

"That's what you think, lady!" he said. "*She* ain't gonna let nobody live here, that old lady. She's been here forever, and she's not aimin' to—"

"You don't understand," I broke in. "This land belongs to me now." I smiled at him. "And you're welcome to hunt 'crawdads' in my creek anytime. . . ."

He was shaking his head, his eyes serious under their thick black lashes. "Creek belongs to the county; this place belongs to her. You'll see, lady!" Then he turned and bounded across the meadow quickly and silently. He reminded me of a fox—alert dark eyes and flashing grace.

Somewhat shaken, I got up, brushed off my blue skirt, put on my shoes, went to Annabel, and started onto the road. But I switched off the engine, got back out of the car, and walked over to the creek bank, just above where I'd dreamed the children were playing a short while ago.

I must have heard Chad down in the creek and imagined the rest, I thought, following a path that led down under the bridge. Both above and below the bridge, the clear water bubbled invitingly over the shallows, glinting brightly in the sun.

Directly under the bridge, however, the water formed a deep green pool where darting minnows, scuttling crawfish, and a graceful striped water snake were little more than ghostly shadows near the bottom. On the far side, the cliffs tapered off leaving only a steep bank. On the side near the driveway, the bank had been eroded so that it leaned out over the water and the rocks below, reaching out with the menacing fingers of twisted elms that clung precariously to the edge and shut out most of the sunlight.

Here I sensed a stillness, an almost eerie waiting, a chill foreboding. I shivered involuntarily and hurried back to the car.

All the way to town, I tried to decide if any of it had been real—the children, Chad. Had it all simply been a strangely vivid dream?

FOUR

"Mr. Roberts," I began without preamble, braving the stares of those in the county court clerk's office, "I owe you an apology. I'm sorry for my flare of temper the other day. My husband says the heat waves in the meadow, combined with shadows, formed a mirage which made me think I saw a house where there's nothing but scrub locusts, a few cedars, and some broom sedge."

He eyed me narrowly. "That's all right, little lady. But you did see that there's no house there?"

"Yes, I did, Mr. Roberts. I'm terribly embarrassed about it. I know I saw a house there that first day, but as my husband says, I guess it was a mirage."

"You can call it that if you want to, Miz Farris. 'Time was, is past; thou canst not it recall. . . .' But from the way you described that house, you saw more than a mirage. That house stood on that property, exactly as you saw it, when I was a boy. I remember it well. We used to pass it on our way to the river. I reckon I was twenty years old before it burned."

He stood there lost in memory while I tried to shake off the chill I felt again. I had forgotten how I'd described the house, and he had instantly recognized it. If I'd seen a mirage, I wouldn't have seen it exactly as the house had looked years ago, as though the building had left its imprint on the space it had occupied for so long. I never had seen that house when it had actually stood on its rise of ground because I had been born long after its burning. But apparently I had seen it in complete and vivid detail just as it had stood.

"Little lady, young Tom came in the other day and had that deed transferred, so I know you bought the place. Told me he might be comin' back here to set up his practice. Tom sure looks a sight like his granddad! Bet he's a good lawyer, too. And the good Lord knows we could use a good lawyer around here, one that ain't as crooked as a railroad roundhouse! But if you don't mind an old man giving you some fatherly advice. . . ." I smiled at him encouragingly. "I say sell that property quick, if you can, and get as far away from that valley as possible. Tom's too young to know much about it, I reckon, but. . . ." He lowered his voice. "There's a curse on that place."

I stared at him. Surely he wasn't serious! But I had doubted his sincerity the other day and been wrong. "What do you mean, Mr. Roberts?" I asked. "Has there been a lot of tragedy there?"

He shook his head. "Oh, there's been tragedy aplenty. More than any one place has a right to, I reckon. But that ain't what I meant. Anyway, I think you'd best forget about Deserter's Creek and build you a nice little ranch house out on the other side of town. The old Farris place was torn down when the interstate went through, but there's some nice land out that way you could build on. That's what I'd do if I was you, which I ain't, and I know you're thinkin' it ain't none of my business, and you're right. But you couldn't pay me to live out there on Deserter's Creek. No, siree! You take my advice, little lady, and let that place alone!"

Mr. Roberts seemed to have a great talent for annoying me, but I decided to humor him this time. So I didn't argue about curses and evil spells, which was what he seemed to be hinting.

"I'll need a builder, wherever I decide to build," I said matter-of-factly. "I'd like your recommendation."

My seeking his advice at last was effective. He abandoned his urgings to sell.

"Well, Miz Farris, there's three or four builders around here, but for my money, Jake Harley is the best of 'em all. He ain't no spring chicken and he may be a mite slower than some, but he's a good sound builder. Any building he puts up for you is likely to be there a good long while, barring acts of God and nature."

I wrote the name and address he gave me on a scrap of paper and put it in my purse. "Thank you, Mr. Roberts. I appreciate your help."

"But not my advice about selling?" He chuckled. "I didn't figure you'd pay it any mind. I could see from the first you had your heart set on that place. Well, little lady, I wish you luck with it. Maybe the curse has blown away by now. It's been a long time."

"I'll invite you and your wife out for supper as soon as we're moved in," I promised impulsively.

"That's a date, little lady, only I ain't got a wife. She's been gone for better'n ten years, God rest her. But I'd be more than glad to come. Only if Lucretia Adams shows up, don't think I'm rude if I leave without taking time to say good-bye!"

I didn't know whether to bite at the obvious bait or not, but my curiosity won. "Who is Lucretia Adams, Mr. Roberts?" I asked warily.

He rested his elbows, praying-mantis-like, on the counter for a long, drawnout tale. "She's the one used to own that place. Some say she burned it down, but I don't see how that could be, since she'd been dead for a number of years when it happened."

"I see," I said untruthfully. "Mr. Roberts, I have to go now. My husband will be waiting. Thanks again for all you've done. I'll be seeing you." *But no sooner than I can help,* I added silently. I didn't have the time or the patience to listen to any ghost-visitation or evil-spirit stories, and I could sense that he was wound up for just that.

Lucretia Adams, indeed! I thought as I climbed into Annabel and started the motor. *That place is mine now, mine and Tom's, and I'd like to see any ghost try to take it away from me!*

Mr. Roberts' suggestion was more powerful than I'd guessed, though, for as I drove home I couldn't help thinking about Lucretia Adams. Had she, too, planned her home in joyful anticipation only to have tragedy after tragedy strike? Then, in desperation, had she burned the house to get rid of it? But, no,

Mr. Roberts had said she was dead when the house burned.

All at once, I wished I hadn't been so hasty and had let Mr. Roberts spin his yarn. It would have been interesting to know something more about my predecessor on Deserter's Creek. There would be time for all that later, though, perhaps at that supper to which I'd already invited Mr. Roberts. Right now, I had to find Jake Harley and get him started on my house.

He wasn't the builder I would have chosen on my own. He was nearing sixty, with a shiny bald head as neatly fringed with iron gray hair as a tonsured monk's. His dark blue eyes bit into mine cynically without apology as I explained from the front stoop of his small brick house what I wanted and who had sent me.

"Old Rob down at the courthouse, you mean?" he asked. "Well, why didn't you say so? Come on in!"

It was the beginning of a strange and complex relationship, but I came to agree with Mr. Roberts' description. Jake Harley certainly was no spring chicken and he was maddeningly slow at times, but he knew what he was doing. The way he measured and remeasured and braced and reinforced what already seemed sturdy made me feel sure that, short of a deliberate act of God, nothing would destroy this house.

Mr. Harley had a crew of one man, plus extras hired for specialized jobs, such as bulldozing.

How I hated that bulldozer! When it first began scraping away broom sedge and locust sprouts, its noise and bulk seemed monstrously alien in the age-old valley, intruders from a foreign time and place. But Mr. Harley pointed out that it would speed things up considerably, so I said no more about it and stayed away from the valley as much as I could until the dozing was done.

Then, Mr. Harley called and asked me to come out there. The dozer had uncovered the old foundation line and he wanted me to see it. Except for one minor variation where an ell branched off from the rest of the house, that age-blackened stone foundation, somewhat scattered but still discernible, fit our new plans as though it had been laid for them! With a slight alteration in the blueprint, we were able to follow the old line.

It seemed good to be building on the old foundation. It gave an added approval, made my house a rightful heir to the land. And it made all the more plausible my half-thought-out theory about the house I had seen and its imprint on this space, though I still didn't understand it.

After the bulldozer operator and Mr. Harley had gone for the day, I knelt in the dirt the dozer had disturbed and picked up a piece of blue and white china, or, rather, a heavy material more like stone-ware. It was curved at the side, and I guessed it had been a bowl. I rubbed the dirt from it. The pattern was of an English street scene, the blue now smudged with time and use and the white cracked in those tiny road-map cracks old china gets.

I could imagine my own dishes broken and buried and my lovely gray house-to-be vanished with time, perhaps only the stone chimney and foundation remaining to show that this valley had been home to someone. Did this other woman, wherever her dispossessed spirit now dwelt, mourn these pitiful remnants of her belongings? I wondered. Would she have approved of me, of Tom, of the house we were building on what had been her foundation? I wished I knew more about her.

Somehow, though, as the house took shape, I felt Lucretia Adams would approve of this building, rebuilding actually, for I tried very hard to make my house as much like the former one as possible.

When something was wrong during the building, I'd feel that odd discontent I'd felt when we were trying to choose a plan, an achy nagging that made me want to cry. Then I'd sit at the edge of the woods, lulled by the sighing of the cedars, my eyes half-closed, half-seeing, half-visualizing, and I would "see" the right way almost as plainly as I'd seen the house that first day.

When I made the corrections—wide oak planks instead of narrow, modern flooring; lighting fixtures that resembled old-time kerosene lamps; cabinets and woodwork aged and mellowed with a blowtorch; a fieldstone fireplace that really worked instead of gas or electric logs—it all felt right again.

"Our house already has a ghost," I told Tom half-jokingly over dinner in our apartment one night. "It's just as if it were hundreds of years old and filled with restless memories."

Tom took a sip of iced tea and set the glass down with a thump. "Don't be ridiculous, Amanda!" he grunted. "There's no such thing as a ghost."

"Why, Tom!" I exclaimed in mock amazement. "Don't you believe in the Holy Ghost?"

"Of course, I do!" he snapped. "But if anything is haunting that place, it could only be evil. Dead Christians don't haunt. They go to be with God."

I didn't argue. Not only was Tom an excellent lawyer, but he knew a lot more about the Scriptures and what Christians, dead or alive, did or didn't do than I probably ever would know. Anyway, I didn't quite believe in my ghost either. But it was fun to invent "ancestors" for my valley home.

I loved wandering over the property, watching the house take shape. When Mr. Harley and his assistant, Dave, were on the job alone, it was peaceful with just the homey sounds of hammer and saw or plane and the natural buzzings and twitterings from the woods and meadow.

The work seemed to go faster if I didn't watch too closely, but they didn't seem to mind my being there. I was careful not to bother them except when something didn't fit my idea of how the house should be built.

Busy selecting drapery material, curtains, and rugs, I hadn't been out to the site for almost a week when Mr. Harley called and asked me to come out the next day to inspect everything before he started taking tools home.

As I drove Annabel out Deserter's Creek Road that golden, early October morning, I fully expected to feel a wild jubilation, or at least a delightful content, when I saw the finished house sitting proudly on its rise of ground. But the moment I turned in the newly graded and graveled drive, I knew it was all wrong. I had that absurd desire to cry. *It was a mistake to disturb this brooding valley, after all,* I thought.

I closed my eyes and recalled the memory of the house as it had appeared that first time I'd seen it. Suddenly I knew what was wrong. That house had been weathered to a soft silvery color that blended in with its surroundings. The pristine white under-coat on the wide weatherboarding of my new house stood out like a slap across the face of the woodland, as alien in this place as the bulldozer had been. It would take years to naturally bring about that soft weathered look. Would the valley and I have to suffer this hideous white intruder until time had mellowed us all? It was too late to ask for stained shingles instead of painted weatherboarding.

All at once, I knew what we could do to "weather" the house. Annabel's wheels scattered gravel into the meadow as I raced to stop Jake Harley from adding a second coat of white, as he was preparing to do as soon as he got his ladder in position.

"I want it painted gray, Mr. Harley!" I called as I set the brake and jumped out of the car.

He turned and stared at me for several seconds. "Gray?" he asked finally. Then he laughed, a little uncertainly. "Good joke, Miz Farris," he said hope-fully. "You saw I had this nice first coat of white on and you thought you'd pull my leg a little about paintin' it gray . . . ?" As I shook my head, his voice trailed off. By now, he'd had quite a bit of experience with my "whims and notions," as he called them. He had learned to give in with a minimum of argument, though it obviously went "against the grain," as he said.

His vivid blue eyes locked into mine, as though trying to see inside the head where such a strange mind boiled continually with ideas purposely calculated to thwart him, to cause him extra work and delay.

"Hold up, Dave!" he called around the corner of the house resignedly. "We gotta paint it gray."

"It's too—oh, I don't know—raw and new looking, I guess," I stammered apologetically. "It just doesn't fit in with the—the landscape."

"I must be getting hard of hearing, Jake!" Dave called from the side of the house. "For a minute there I thought you said we hadda paint the house gray. What did you say, Jake?"

"That's what I said! We gotta paint it gray! The boss lady here says it don't fit the landscape."

I heard Dave's long, blown-out sigh all the way around to the front of the house. "I knew it!" he muttered. "The minute I seen that car comin' down the road, I knew it meant trouble!"

"I'm sorry, Mr. Harley," I said. "Really I am." I felt awful insisting on this last-minute change, but it wasn't a change really. I had never thought of the house as anything but gray, but I couldn't remember saying anything about it to Mr. Harley. It was all my fault, but I had only to look at that unnatural whiteness to know I was right about the color. It should be weathered to gray, but gray paint would be better than white. "I'll pay extra for the added work," I added, hoping Tom wouldn't mind too much.

"It's your money," he said. "You go pick up the paint and bring it back. I can finish these shutters while you're gone. Or do you want them gray, too?" His voice was carefully bland, but his eyes said he no longer would be surprised at anything I might request of him.

"Oh, no, Mr. Harley, white shutters will be fine. And I'll be back in a jiffy with the paint. Where do I get it?"

He told me, and I hurried to Annabel. I was beginning to feel better now. The house would be gray, and it wouldn't be long before we could move in. A few more days at the most and we would be living in our new home! I had no reason to believe that our life here on Deserter's Creek would be anything but happy.

FIVE

Crossing the bridge with the last of our clothes and Tom's grandparents' Seth Thomas clock, I stopped Annabel on the bridge and sat savoring the soft silvery gray of the house with its white shutters and trim framed by the flaming oranges and reds of the maples and oaks behind it, all wrapped in the incredible blue of an October sky.

I'd never been happier in my life, not even on my wedding day, for now I had both Tom and the home I'd always wanted. I glanced down at the murky green of the creek, stained brown at the edges by the fallen sycamore leaves from the white limbs that reached out over the water. Suddenly, I felt a strange reluctance to intrude on this ancient valley.

"Jake Harley would have called that a 'notion,' " I told myself aloud, "and one that's several thousand dollars too late!" Laughing, I pressed down on the accelerator, eased Annabel up the lane, and parked beside the moving van.

"Over there is where I'll build my dog kennel, Amanda," Tom called as I got out of the car at the end of the stone walk. I knew our house meant less to him than it did to me, for he never had lacked a home when he was growing up. But he had been on his own for a number of years, living in dormitories and apartments, and I could tell he was pleased that we had a place of our own at last.

I walked over to stand beside him, only half listening to his plans, loving the protective feel of the hard-muscled arm he placed around my shoulders, loving everything about him and the day.

A bit later Tom went back to town in his Chrysler to turn in the apartment key and to get the last of the precious law books he'd inherited from his grandfather. For the first time, I worked in the house alone. Even when I had cleaned the house after the builders were finished, Tom had insisted on coming with me.

"Are you going to quit work and stay home with me all the time?" I had teased.

He had smiled, but his eyes were serious. "I'll soon have my office here in town, I think. There's an office being vacated over the bakery that I might be able to get. Anyway, after we move in, maybe it won't seem so deserted out here."

I knew what he meant, but I loved being out here all by ourselves. Already I had spent several afternoons here before the house was started. No one had come near the place except for a few fishermen on their way to the river. I'd never encountered anyone on our property except Chad Palmer, and I had seen him only once. I still thought he might have been a dream.

I worked on contentedly, straightening, arranging,

trying various combinations of furniture and accessories. Most of our things were carefully bought and well-loved antiques, or reproductions of colonial or Shaker styles that fit in perfectly with the house.

Hearing the front door slam and footsteps cross the entry, I took one last satisfied look around the living room and hurried out to meet Tom.

"Hello, darl. . . . " My voice faded. No one was in the hall. A packing box sat where I'd left it, filled with the newspapers that had been packed around the ashtrays, pictures, and candle holders I had just arranged in the room behind me. Nothing else was there at all. Yet I was sure I had heard that door and the footsteps.

"Tom?" I called. My voice echoed eerily through the house. I opened the front door and looked out. Annabel sat alone in the driveway. The Chrysler was nowhere in sight. I felt a chill of apprehension. Quickly I turned and went back into the bedroom. Nothing. I searched the entire house, upstairs and down, but I was alone.

I had a creepy feeling for a few moments; then I shrugged and went back to my unpacking, too busy and too satisfied with my new home to give it much thought. I had that comfortable feeling of being, not only where I wanted to be, but where I was wanted as well. I had been seeking that feeling for a long time.

By the time I heard Tom's car in the driveway, I had forgotten the incident, and I didn't recall it until the next Sunday.

Tom went back to Lexington alone to attend church. Although usually I accompanied him, more to be with him than for any devoutness on my part,

I had used a slight headache as an excuse to stay home. I didn't really mind going to church; it just meant a lot less to me than it did to Tom.

I was home alone, as I had been the day we moved in. This time I was in the bedroom smoothing the bedspread, with its white and yellow daisies on a blue field, over the pillows and tucking it in between the spindles of our cherry spool bed. I was thinking of how I had found this prized possession in a cluttered little antique-junk shop and had carried most of it out in a bushel basket! Every spindle had been out of the frame, and the frame itself had been broken in places. But when the antique restorer had finished with it, our bed was a masterpiece of polished cherry wood, as solid as a new bed.

When I heard the front door open and shut, I glanced up into the hall, one hand poised over the last wrinkle in the spread. *Tom is back early and I haven't even started dinner!* I moved over to the doorway. No one seemed to be in the hall. Then I heard the floor creak, that one misfitting board near the kitchen. I could see the doorway plainly; no one was there. Yet, someone's weight had creaked that board. I was sure of it.

I hurried into the kitchen, fear hovering at the base of my neck, expecting to find the same eerie emptiness I had found the other day. I gasped when I saw the blue-clad figure standing with his back to me, looking out the kitchen window.

He turned slowly and looked directly at me. His dark eyes were sunken and feverish looking. I had seen eyes like that before, with that same despair and hopelessness. I felt a rush of relief mixed with annoyance at Tom. Did we have to share our first Sunday in our new home with one of his derelicts? Couldn't we have one week to ourselves before he began making a skid-row hotel here on Deserter's Creek? And it really wasn't like Tom to leave me alone with his strays.

Still, the man was so painfully thin and ravaged looking that I couldn't hurt his feelings. I would just have to make the best of it. I smiled at him and went to plug in the coffeepot.

He stared at me despairingly for several seconds more, then turned and went out the back door without a word. Quickly I followed him to the door, wondering anxiously if he were bent on self-destruction and what I should do about it. His eyes had been so haunted!

I could see him plainly crossing the shadow of the house. If he had gone into the woods, I still would have been able to see him for several yards before the trees and underbrush thickened. But when he ran into the bright sunlight, I caught one gleam of reflected light from auburn hair and gold buttons, and then he was gone, as though he had been a mist the sun had burned away!

I leaned against the doorjamb, my legs suddenly too weak to hold me erect. Again, I scanned the yard and woods from the doorway. The sunlight streamed in an unbroken line across the trees at the edge of the woods.

"This is incredible!" I whispered. Yet, I *had* seen someone. I knew I hadn't been dreaming this time. I was positive of that.

I felt bone tired, and my head had begun to ache terribly. I shivered with a sudden chill. Carefully holding onto the kitchen table, then the doorjambs and walls, I made my way to the bedroom. . . .

. . . The high old walnut bed creaked as I collapsed across it, burying my cold face in the patchwork quilt with its one scratchy block under my cheek. That block made from the white wool of my wedding shawl. . . .

The slamming of the front door woke me. For an instant, I didn't know where I was. Then my eyes focused on the familiar blue and yellow spread between the spools of the cherry bed. A man's footsteps were coming toward the bedroom. Fear crawled down my spine.

"What's wrong, sweetheart?" Tom asked sympathetically. "Headache worse?"

"Oh, Tom, thank God, it's you!"

"Well, who were you expecting?" he asked in surprise. "Say, something *is* wrong! You're as pale as a ghost!"

I shivered at his choice of words. "Tom, I don't know. I don't understand any of it. It's so weird!" I told him about the man in the kitchen and his disappearing act in the backyard.

Tom stood with his head thrown back, his eyes narrowed in thought. Finally, he began to laugh. His big blondness and his hearty laughter seemed out of place, hateful. . . . But that was ridiculous! This was Tom, the man I loved with all my being. My experience with the dark-eyed stranger in the kitchen must have shaken me even more than I'd realized.

"Amanda," Tom said patiently, "you must have had a dream. You made the bed, lay down on it, and dozed off. That explains—"

"No, Tom," I interrupted. "It wasn't a dream. I'm sure of that. I only lay down afterward. Tom, if you could have seen that poor man's eyes! He looked like his last hope was gone."

Tom was shaking his head, a slight smile still playing about his lips. "Poor Amanda! You've had to put up with too many strays, haven't you? No wonder you dream about them! We were lucky this one disappeared, I guess, or we'd be having company for Sunday dinner. By the way, we are having some, aren't we? Sunday dinner, I mean."

I wasn't so easily distracted from my certainty that this morning's experience had been real. "Tom, when I fell across the bed, why was it an antique monstrosity spread with a patchwork quilt? I can even remember the feel of one of the squares against my face, a scratchy white woolen piece." I didn't mention the wedding shawl. That simply was too bizarre.

I had been married in the summer in a thin white satin dress with a fingertip veil. There certainly had been no woolen shawl about my shoulders! I couldn't imagine where that idea had come from, but then I had no idea where the patchwork quilt and walnut bed had come from—or the distraught dark-eyed man. And more puzzling, where had he gone?

"Amanda!" Tom's hands were on my shoulders, forcing me to look at him. "You had a dream. There is no other explanation for the things you're saying. Surely you realize that!"

I was still convinced that it had not been a dream. If so, then either I was crazy or I had just encountered a ghost in my new kitchen. I didn't like either of those alternatives.

"I guess you're right," I agreed reluctantly. "It must have been a dream, but it seemed so real!" I got up from the bed. "I'll start dinner." I smoothed the blue and yellow spread where I had wrinkled it and started into the kitchen.

"I'll be out by the woods on the north side," Tom said, following me. "That's where I'm building the dog kennel. Joe Johnson's got me a dog lined up."

"Good!" I answered from the freezer. "Isolated as we are out here, we could use a good watchdog."

Tom laughed. "Don't count on the gallant Black Night for that, sweetheart!"

I turned and looked at him. "With a name like Black Knight, he should be bold and fearless," I teased.

"Not Black *K-n-i-g-h-t,* but *N-i-g-h-t,*" he corrected. "As in 'black as midnight.' But you know how beagles are for making friends. Scratch behind those heavy ears and instant buddy! You'll love Black Night. He's floppy-earred and bench-legged with a broad tan head and black blanket. He has tan freckles on his four white feet and across his nose, and Joe says he can run the fur off a rabbit without even breathing hard!"

I love you, I thought, watching his eyes light up like a small boy's as he told me about the dog. "Well, anyway, he'll be company for me when you're not here," I said, following Tom into the hall with some frozen steaks in my hand, reluctant to be alone again.

He studied me seriously. "You're not getting jumpy out here in the country, are you, Manda? Are you sorry we built the house here?"

"Of course not!" I answered quickly, but my laughter was forced, and as Tom shut the door behind him, I found myself glancing into the kitchen before going to the stove for my iron skillet to fry the steaks. I could still see those haunted eyes that had sought mine so desperately. What had they asked of me? What had they wanted that I had not been able to supply? Help of some kind, surely, but what? What terrible burden had caused that look of despair? Or did some awful guilt drive him?

"Forget it!" I told myself sternly. "It was a dream." It had to be. As Tom had said, there simply was no other explanation. And hadn't I dreamed the children down in the creek, and possibly even Chad Palmer?

But I think I knew, even then, that the dream explanation, though the most acceptable, was not the right one.

SIX

I loved Black Night the minute I saw Tom taking him out of the car on Monday evening. He was as black as a moonless night, with tan markings and white freckled paws broad enough to cover a knee of my jeans as he reared up for me to pat him. I scratched him behind the ears and rubbed his throat, and he went into an ecstasy of moans and wrigglings and was my instant buddy, as Tom had predicted.

Tom chained the dog near the doghouse he had set up by the woods, "just till he gets used to the place," he promised at the dog's and my reproachful looks. He put food and water nearby and we left him for the night.

I was drawn outside about midmorning the next day by Black Night's frantic barking, which turned to an unearthly howling as I opened the front door. I could see nothing that would have sent him into such a frenzy.

"What's wrong, boy?" I called. Black Night howled

twice more, then looked down toward the creek, tucked his tail between his legs, hung his head, and ran inside the doghouse. I turned just in time to see a dark-haired woman in a long dark dress vanish over the creek bank. But though I stood there several minutes longer, I saw nothing more of her.

I went out to the kennel and after some coaxing, got Black Night to come out of his house. I praised and patted him, told him he was very brave to have given that warning bark. "You're going to make a fine watchdog," I told him several times. Before long I had talked him out of his shame at having hidden in the doghouse. He gave me a wet kiss on the cheek, and I hugged him and went back to the house, convinced our trespasser had been some city woman who had been out for a drive and had decided to gather some leaves or berries by the creek.

Two days later, I saw her again. This time she was crossing the garden space, her full dark dress sweeping over the ground Tom had marked off for our spring garden.

Black Night had been running loose for two days and though he usually parked on the front step waiting for a handout, he was nowhere to be seen now. I saw our trespasser only because I was on my way out to burn trash in the burner near the garden.

I set the overloaded trash basket down and called, "Hello, there!" She gave no sign of having heard me. "Hello?" I called again. "Can I help you?"

She did not alter her pace. When she reached the woods on the other side of the garden plot, she simply disappeared into them without a backward glance.

"Well!" I huffed, as I struck a match and lit the paper I'd dumped into the burner. "You surely are a friendly trespasser!" But maybe that was why she had pretended not to hear me—she was ashamed of trespassing. But why did she come onto the property at all if she were that sensitive about it? And who was she anyway?

Finally, I shrugged it off and went back to my housecleaning, but I was still fuming when Tom came home.

"She would have been welcome to a winter bouquet if she'd just asked me!" I told him. "But I'll bet that old bag would have a fit if she caught me picking flowers or leaves out of her yard without permission!"

Tom kissed me, then said, "I know, sweetheart. People think once outside the city limits it's all free for the taking. Say, talking about ecology—which we almost were," he said with a laugh, "I came across a book the other day about a new way of gardening using organic materials, no chemicals, no artificial fertilizers, everything natural—"

"Tom," I interrupted, "that must have been the way Adam gardened! It can't be all that 'new.' "

He grinned sheepishly. "But it's new to the age of the atom, sweetheart! Who, these days, would dream of doing anything simply and naturally if he can tangle it up in computer tape and douse it with chemicals?"

I laughed with him, and we spent the evening discussing our future spring garden and starting a compost heap for fertilizer. I forgot about my wandering lady.

The next day, our second Friday here, I saw Chad again. *At least he's not a dream,* I thought with satisfaction as I watched him coming across the meadow.

He was as dirty as the last time I had seen him and nearly as naked. His feet were thrust into dirty, ragged tennis shoes, and he had changed his shorts for full-length jeans, though they barely reached his ankles and were so threadbare they hardly hid his skin. His loose shirt, with only two buttons left, was such a rusty gray-brown that I had no idea what color it had been originally. The sleeves had been cut off just above his elbows, the raw edges left to ravel.

"Hello, Chad," I greeted, forcing back the impulse to reach out and smooth his shaggy hair.

He stood staring at the house.

"How do you like it?" I asked.

He looked me squarely in the eye. "You seen her yet?"

"Who?"

"That old lady. The one what owns this place."

"Now see here, Chad," I began angrily. Then ashamed of myself for letting this ragged urchin get to me, I forced my voice to a calmer tone. "I told you that *I* own this place now, and I want you to stop hinting around and tell me exactly what you mean!"

He studied me for a moment, then let an impudent grin spread over his face. "Come up into the woods and I'll show you something." He started up the slope, arrogantly confident that I would follow. I don't know if I went more out of curiosity or because of the feeling that I should humor him until I found out just how unbalanced he really was.

I soon put such thoughts aside, for I had all I could

do to keep his slender figure in sight through the trees. He climbed the wooded slope swiftly and almost silently, effortlessly choosing the easier paths, while I struggled through the undergrowth and contended with rock ledges and low-hanging branches. I finally caught up with him because he had stopped in a grove of cedars and stood leaning against a giant white oak, its towering upper branches lost in a sea of flaming leaves.

Chad didn't even seem out of breath. When I could breathe without gasping, I said, "OK, Chad, I'm ready to go on."

"This is it," he answered, waving one grimy hand to indicate the general area under the oak.

The autumn woods were dim and still. After scrutinizing the area, I could see what Chad meant. No fence or dividing line separated the area from the surrounding trees. Just a few stones were scattered beneath the spreading limbs of the white oak. We were in the clump of cedars I often heard sighing in the wind. The cedars had invaded the graveyard and had overgrown it so that they towered over the graves, even now, moaning softly, in the breeze.

One very old stone was embedded in the trunk of the tree Chad leaned against. And one of them, I noticed in surprise, was a real carved headstone with an inscription hidden beneath years of accumulated lichen and dirt. It was a beautiful thing carved in the shape of a tree stump, weathered to gray, blending with the trees. On its top, a playful squirrel was captured forever in stone. *A stone for an outdoorsman,* I thought, *someone like Tom.*

The tangled canes of a rosebush had twisted themselves around it. I reached out to touch them, wondering if it was a wild rosebush or if someone had planted it there.

"It's the same as that white rosebush under your window." Chad answered my unspoken question.

The other stones, like the one in the tree, were merely rocks set on end to mark the graves. All of them were old and moss-covered, nearly hidden beneath a tangled growth of honeysuckle and periwinkle vines.

Another fifty years, I thought morbidly, *and the honeysuckle and other tangled growths will claim the graveyard. There'll be no trace of the graves or their markers, and nothing at all left to show that these people once had lived in this valley.* It was a depressing thought, and suddenly I wanted to do something for these unknown people who perhaps had loved this valley long before I was born.

The least I could do, I decided, would be to cut back the weeds, tangled vines, and rose canes and clean the encrusted dirt from the carved stone so that the inscription could be read. I reached down into the matted vines and pulled a handful of them away from one of the stones. The long, trailing tendrils broke off near the ground.

"They'll just come up thicker than ever," Chad warned pessimistically.

"All right," I snapped, suddenly tired of his self-appointed superiority, "what do you recommend to get this graveyard back to a decent state?"

He shrugged imperturbably and studied the area. "A grubbin' hoe, maybe, and some pruners for a start."

"Sorry, I'm fresh out of both those articles." I still felt cross and more than a little tired, maybe from a strange depression I couldn't seem to shake off. Sinking down on one of the larger, rough-cut stones, I wondered if it was any use to clean this place up. Much as I hated to admit it, Chad was right. It would all grow back, and I wouldn't always be around to clean it up again.

"I wouldn't sit in those vines, if I was you," Chad said casually. "Copperheads. This woods is full of 'em."

I jumped up. Snakes of any kind were hardly my favorite creatures, not to mention the hateful, venomous copperhead. As a matter of fact, I wished Chad hadn't. Now my wooded paradise held unseen serpents under every ledge and bush. I wasn't sure I had the courage to grope into this jungle of vines and leaves. I was becoming reconciled to the fact that I had no tools with which to clear the graveyard.

"We've got a grubbin' hoe and pruners you can borry, if you want to," Chad offered.

I searched his gamin face for signs of guile, but it was as innocently blank as any face I had ever seen. Chad was quick, though. I felt sure he had read my cowardly thoughts.

"I'll go get the tools," he said. My suspicions were confirmed when I caught an impish grin as he turned to leave.

"Thanks!" I answered dryly.

He disappeared gracefully in a matter of seconds, leaving me alone in the dim and rustling woods. I'd seen him wandering this valley barefoot not long ago,

I suddenly remembered. Either his estimate of copperheads had been exaggerated for my benefit or he had no fear of them.

"Little imp!" I muttered, determined to wait here for him if it killed me. And I wasn't at all sure it wouldn't, from fear alone. I forced snakes out of my mind. Then, hoping to be able to read the inscription, I cautiously began pulling vines away from the carved tree stump.

I didn't quite know what to think of Chad or of his mother, if he had one, for letting him roam around so ragged and dirty. And shouldn't he have been in school today?

The inscription was so encrusted with lichen and dirt that I gave up my efforts and sat back down to wait for Chad. I didn't know he was approaching until he dropped the grubbing hoe behind me, nearly scaring me into the next world. I caught the remains of a sly grin on his face when I turned angrily. He wasn't looking at me, of course. He knelt in the "copperhead laden" vines and fitted the rusty pruners around a thick Virginia Creeper stem. I picked up the hoe and began a futile attempt at chopping a mat of honeysuckle.

Chad stopped to watch me for a few seconds, then grinned up at me. "Here, you take the pruners," he offered, "and I'll use the hoe."

A little shamefaced, I traded with him, but the expert way he uprooted the stubborn vines convinced me it had been a good trade. *He seems strong for his size, in spite of his thinness,* I thought as I stood fingering the worn handles of the pruners. I felt

carved initials under my fingers without really thinking about them, but Chad must have thought I was
wondering about the letters and the man who had
carved them.

"Belonged to my dad," he said.

I took a good look at them then. The *TP* had been
cut deeply by a sure hand into the hard wood of the
handle. Chad held up the hoe, and I saw matching
letters on its handle.

"Belonged?" I questioned softly.

"Yeah. He's dead," Chad answered matter-of-factly.
"Mama gave me all his tools." He looked down toward
the house. "*She* killed him!"

"Your mama?" I gasped.

He looked at me scornfully out of those dark eyes.
"Not Mama! That old lady what owns . . . what used
to own this place," he corrected himself quickly. "Lucretia somebody. She was some kin to my dad on his
mother's side, Mama says. But that didn't stop her
from killin' him."

I murmured, "I'm sorry," and busied myself with
the pruners. We worked for some time in silence, my
thoughts searching for a way to explain how Lucretia
Adams could have killed a man who surely hadn't
been born until long after her death.

"Did you know my dad?" Chad asked suddenly.

I glanced up at him, but he was busy grubbing
vines and piling them to be carried away.

"Why, no, Chad, I didn't," I began, "but if he was
anything like—"

"Then how did you know his name?"

"His name?" I repeated stupidly. Then, remembering the initials, I took a wild guess. "Was it Tom? My husband's name is Tom. Maybe I mentioned him and you thought. . . ."

Chad was shaking his head stubbornly. "Tarrellton. You called me Tarrellton and that was his name and Mama says I look just like him."

I stood up abruptly, letting the pruners fall. "Tarrellton?" I whispered.

He was watching me closely. "You *did* know him! When you saw me, you thought it was him."

"No, Chad, I didn't! It's just that I. . . ." I stopped in confusion. How could I explain that I had been having a dream about someone's name I had never known, and it had turned out to be the name of a man whose son just happened to be standing over me when I awoke? Was it some weird mental telepathy that I had picked up from Chad's own thoughts that day?

"Chad," I said simply, "I have no idea where I got that name. I was having a dream, and the name seemed to be a part of the dream. I've never known anyone by the name of Tarrellton."

He nodded as though he understood about dreams and went back to his work. There was a sulky look about his mouth, though. Or was it merely disappointment at having lost what he had hoped was a link with his dead father?

All at once, I—the girl with no mother—felt a great sympathy for this lonely little boy with no father. I didn't dare show it, for he was as prickly as one of the green briars I was wrestling, every bit as prickly as I once had been.

I watched him as he worked. He was thorough and

quick. When he had a pile of vines and brush, with both bare arms he gathered them up, thorns and all, and carried them off to a small gully he had found. He worked steadily and without complaint.

I'll need help, I thought, *first with this project and later with mowing the lawn and other odd jobs.* If I could persuade Chad to work for me, it might prove mutually beneficial. If what he was wearing indicated the state of his wardrobe, he could use some new clothes and, no doubt, had other needs at which I could only guess.

I straightened my aching back and looked around the graveyard. We had cleared the grave with the carved stone and had made inroads on the others.

"I'm quitting now, Chad!" I called, exhausted, unaccustomed to the heavy labor.

He hurried back from the gully. "Ain't you gonna clean the stone?"

"Not today!" I said with a laugh. "I'm worn to a frazzle already! The stone can wait. Let's go fix us a snack. OK?"

The dark eyes studied me curiously. "Don't you even want to know about her? This is her husband's grave. Maybe she killed him, too. But she killed my dad as sure as I'm standin' here, and you'll prob'ly be next. She kills everybody who tries to take her precious place away from her!" He was practically raving, and I stared at him in dismay.

"Chad, what are you talking about? That's the second time today you've. . . . What do you mean, she killed your father? That woman has been dead since before your father was born! She couldn't possibly. . . . Chad, that's crazy!" I bit my lip. I hadn't meant to say that. I was afraid it was too close to the truth.

Chad bent down and carefully selected a small stone. I had a moment's fear that he might throw it at me, but he seemed to be taking his anger out on the gravestone. He was scrubbing at it furiously with the rock he had picked up, rubbing back and forth over the carved letters.

I bit back a protest at this defacing of the ancient marker when I noticed that the scrubbing was clearing the inscription of lichen and dirt, making it readable. Filling in a couple of illegible letters, I read:

JOEL HARRISON ADAMS
beloved husband of
Lucretia T. Adams
May 5, 1835–July 17, 1864

*. . . He that heareth my word, and believeth
on him that sent me, hath everlasting life,
and shall not come into condemnation;
but is passed from death unto life.*
John 5:24

I was right, I thought. He'd been a Civil War victim, or at least the dates fit. The stone did not indicate which army he had served with, if any.

Suddenly I wondered where his wife was buried and why Lucretia T. Adams did not rest here beside her "beloved husband." I asked Chad about it.

"Oh, she's buried over in the churchyard," he answered. "But she ain't nowhere near my dad!" His voice had a sudden energy in it. I could see hatred in his eyes. He really did believe Lucretia Adams had killed his father.

Maybe if I take him to her grave and prove she was buried there, I thought, *and show him that the dates make it impossible for her to have been around when Tarrellton Palmer met his death, Chad will believe it.* In any case, I wanted to see her stone and whatever might be carved on it. Her story had begun to grip my imagination.

"Take me to the churchyard, Chad," I coaxed. "I'd like to see her grave. And your father's," I added to persuade him.

Chad shrugged his thin shoulders. "If you want to."

We stopped by the house long enough to wash up and eat some cookies and drink a couple of Cokes. Then we climbed into the car and drove up the road about two miles to the little white country church I passed every time I traveled to or from town.

As we left Annabel, I noticed that the tall, narrow frame building had no fence dividing it from the graveled parking lot on its left and the graveyard on its right. *It's been kept up well if it's been here since the middle 1800's,* I thought as I let Chad pass me so he could lead the way. The only sign of deterioration was the empty cupolalike bell tower that no longer had its bell.

"My dad is here next to the church," Chad said, stopping beside a plain square granite marker to the right of the building. "They almost didn't have room for him, but Mama wanted him close to home. Anyway, she didn't have the money to buy a grave somewheres else. They let her bury him beside the walk that goes around to the side door. All his kinfolk are buried here somewheres."

Dutifully, I admired the marker with the name "Tarrellton Palmer" and the dates of his birth and death. Then I noticed the words carved beneath them:

> *Let us eat and drink;*
> *for tomorrow we shall die.*
> Isaiah 22:13

I suppressed a shudder. How different those bitter words were from those on Joel Harrison Adams' stone! I tried to recall the inscription that went something like "He that believeth on me hath everlasting life . . . is passed from death unto life. . . ."

"Brother Jimmy here at the church says my mama shouldn't have put that on there," Chad interrupted my thoughts. "My dad was a believer. But Mama says it don't make no difference 'cause he's dead anyway."

I searched my mind frantically for one of Tom's verses that might bring comfort to this strange little boy, but I couldn't think of any. Chad stood looking somberly at the stone, then bent and picked up a pint jar with the dried brown remains of flowers in it. He flung it over the fence that bordered the whole property, and I shuddered as I heard it shatter against what must have been a graveyard for flower containers.

"You miss him a lot, don't you?" I said finally, watching him polish the stone with the tail of his shirt.

He shrugged off my sympathy brusquely. "I barely remember him. I was just a little kid when he died."

Then he turned serious, almost fanatical, eyes upon me. "How come I can see her but I can't never see him?" he asked.

I thought I knew what he meant, but I hesitated to go into that question too deeply, so I simply said, "I don't know, Chad."

"I didn't mean to! It was her. You gotta believe that!"

"What? What must I believe, Chad?"

"Not you," he muttered. "Come on. The old woman's grave is over that way. All those stones over there are real old."

I followed him, picking my way carefully among the low footstones that were all but hidden in the tall grass that appeared to have been cut with a mowing blade rather than with a lawn mower. Even so, I tripped several times as I tried to read inscriptions on the headstones.

Chad was impatient to be going now that we had visited his father's grave. He certainly had no interest in paying respects to the dead woman he believed had killed his father.

Almost to the far fence, he stopped and pointed to a slender obelisk of white marble, a beautifully cut stone about six feet tall.

In large letters the stone read simply: A D A M S. But carved in each of the four sides was more lettering. Remembering Chad's way of cleaning the stone in the woods, I picked up a small rock and began scrubbing at the letters on the base of the obelisk, expecting to find something like "Beloved wife of Joel Harrison Adams" engraved there. But as I worked my way around the stone, I saw that each of the four sides held a different name and date.

Was it the common grave of four people? Apparently it was. From the placement of the foot markers, they each had been buried at a different side of the stone. Then I noticed the dates of death. They all had died on November 21, 1865!

What tragedy took all of them in a single day? I wondered. *Were they also war victims?*

The inscription on the side of the stone facing the church read: "Lucretia Tarrellton Oct. 12, 1836–Nov. 21, 1865." Quickly I calculated that she had been twenty-nine years old at the time of her death.

Moving to the left, I saw the inscription "Harrison Jan. 3, 1854–Nov. 21, 1865." This must have been the son of Lucretia and Joel Adams, nearly twelve years old.

The back inscription read: "Susannah Apr. 17, 1858–Nov. 21, 1865." This would have been their seven-year-old daughter.

The side of the stone facing the road read: "Tarrellton Apr. 14, 1855–Nov. 21, 1865." Another son, going on eleven years old.

Why were they buried here in the churchyard, I wondered, *while the children's father, Lucretia's husband, was in the woods behind my house?*

Suddenly I felt as if all the breath had been knocked out of me. Those names—Susannah, Harrison, and Tarrellton—were the names of the children I had dreamed were playing down in the creek!

"I'm losing my mind!" I whispered. But not even insanity could explain how I had dreamed, or imagined, three names that I had later discovered on a gravestone in this churchyard. Stranger still, they were the children of the people who had once owned our land, children who must have played in that creek many times. I couldn't have seen the stone and sub-consciously remembered the names to give to my dream children, because I had never been here before and the stone was barely visible from the road. Three of the four sides weren't visible at all from there.

I looked around wildly. Chad was gone. Or had he been here at all? Was he, too, a figment of my twisted imaginings? Was I here in this country graveyard with its narrow white church, or was it all something con-jured up by my suddenly erratic mind?

I stumbled over footstones, falling to my knees several times in my haste to get back to Annabel. As I drove past the graveyard, though I could not possi-bly see it from here, the name Tarrellton wavered defiantly before my eyes, as mockingly defiant as the black-eyed boy himself, as I had envisioned him in the creek that day.

I don't know how I got back to the house safely. When I looked out later, Annabel was parked as usual in the driveway, but I actually had no memory of having driven home.

By the time Tom came home, I had composed myself by simply refusing to think about it anymore. I wasn't sure I should tell Tom about it, after the way he had reacted to the incident last Sunday, so I kept putting it off.

After supper, Tom lit a fire in the stone fireplace. I curled up on the braided rug and sat staring into the flames while he poured over the inevitable case history. Finally he broke into my thoughts.

"You were a hundred miles away!" he teased, grin-ning down at me.

"Years," I corrected absently.

"What?"

"A hundred years away, not miles. Her name was Lucretia, Tom. Lucretia Tarrellton Adams."

"Amanda, I have no idea what or whom you are talking about," he said with a laugh.

I told him about the two graveyards and the strange marker with its four names that were exactly the names I had given previously to my dream children. This time he didn't laugh, but seemed seriously concerned as he sat pondering the evidence. Then he gave me his verdict.

"I don't know. I suppose it could be some form of mental telepathy. Somehow you must have picked up the boy's thoughts."

"That could explain Tarrellton," I agreed. "But what about Susannah and Harrison?"

He thought that over briefly. "That kid must have seen that gravestone many times. He could have come from there that afternoon with the names fresh on his mind when he stood over you, or maybe you read those names on something at the county court-house."

He got up and replaced his book in the bookcase beside the fireplace, then reached a hand down to help me up. "Come on, sweetheart. We'll pray about all this and forget the weird manifestations, and get to bed early. I want to go squirrel hunting at the crack of dawn. You don't have to get up when I do. I'll just grab a cup of coffee and some toast when I get back. Bet you I bring home a squirrel for supper. Bet?"

I smiled absently and took the hand he offered,

my thoughts still on the graveyard as he pulled me to my feet and into his arms. Even as I automatically returned his kiss, I was thinking that Tom hadn't explained how Chad could have read the inscriptions on the stone earlier when I had been able to read them only after I had cleaned them this afternoon.

SEVEN

I heard the back door shut as Tom left the house early the next morning. When I woke again, the sun was shining in across my face. . . .

. . . *I had dressed and was making the bed when I heard the soft rumble of horses' hooves in the deep yellow dust of the lane. There were several horses and they were galloping.*

Hurriedly I gave the patchwork quilt one last smoothing motion and started to the door. Then some instinctive caution made me edge over to the bedroom window and peer out the side of the white ruffled curtains. My heart lurched with fear. A half-dozen blue-uniformed men on horseback were at the near end of the lane. One of them held the reins of a saddled, riderless horse. Leather creaked as their leader dismounted.

How long has Joel been gone? *I wondered in sudden*

panic. An hour? No more. The sun is scarcely higher now than it was when he left. *"God, help me to keep them here!"* I prayed as I ran to the door.

Remembering just in time that I must appear unworried, normal, I removed the side combs from my hair and smoothed it, and ran my hands down the hips of my crisp dark blue print dress. How it had managed to keep its crispness through this morning's ordeal I couldn't imagine. I felt as if all the starch had been taken out of me, leaving me as limp and spiritless as a wet cloth. Yet the white clover blossoms with their green leaves on the dark blue background of the dress were fresh and real looking.

The captain—I could see now that's what he was—had come to the front step. He paused—one foot on the step, the other on the ground—when he saw me.

The simple sounds, scents, and sights of that hot July morning are burned into my brain like a brand. My nostrils stung with the acrid scent of horse sweat mingled with dust and leather. The creak of saddles as the men shifted on their horses, the jingle of the gear of the riderless bay horse as he tossed his head— all seemed unnaturally loud in the sudden silence. Above it all I could smell the muskiness of the creek at low water mark. Nausea rose in my throat.

"Pardon the intrusion, ma'am . . . ," the captain began, baring his sandy head and smiling gravely at me. *His hair was almost the color of my husband's, but he was very young, with eyes as blue as the July sky. Also, he was very tired. It showed in the circles under his eyes and the weary droop of his shoulders. "We're looking for Corporal Joel Adams, ma'am,*

and . . . uh . . . well, ma'am, I'm afraid we'll have to search the house."

My mind scrambled frantically like a caged animal. I must keep them here as long as possible, give him a chance to make it back to camp on his own, voluntarily. They'll never believe he is on his way back if they catch him now. They'll shoot first and ask questions later.

"Come in, Captain," I invited, thankful that I'd taken the children to their grandparents yesterday after Joel had come home. There was no one else here to betray him accidentally. *"I'll fetch some fresh water for your men. They must be hot and thirsty."*

He seemed a bit taken aback, but after a moment's hesitation, he stepped inside. I took the wooden bucket from the shelf and went to the spring below the creek bank, Joel's words this morning before he had left echoing through my mind: *"I can't shoot my friends and neighbors, Lu, no matter what color uniform they're wearing now. Why, Jed and I grew up together! When I looked out there and saw him. . . . But the colonel is fair and understanding. If I go back, as you say, maybe he will send me somewhere far from Kentucky or give me something to do besides killing. You know how I hate to kill anything! But to kill a man. . . . Lord, Lu, I just can't do it!"*

Joel had covered his face with his hands, and I had longed to take him in my arms and comfort him, tell him he needn't go back, that he could stay here with me and forget the war. But the war must be ended. Our children could not grow up amid all *this turmoil and hatred. And Joel must not be branded a deserter.*

In the end, I'd won and he had gone back. Or at least he had started. I never had loved him more.

Now back from the spring, I set the bucket of cold, clear water down in the yard and handed the gourd dipper to one of the men.

"That's mighty kind of you, ma'am," the captain said from the doorway. "Under the circumstances."

I prayed fervently that Joel was putting miles between us and that this sharp-eyed soldier would not see through my ruse. I knew I must not overplay the sympathy role and make him suspicious. As it was, he was studying me intently, his eyes almost fanatical under their sandy brows.

"I'd do as much for a dog, Captain," I said. "However, you do represent my army."

"Your husband is a deserter, ma'am. I suppose you know that. I don't guess it would do any good to ask if he's been here?"

I stared at him coldly.

"I thought not. Ma'am, I'm sorry, but we have orders to search here for him."

I nodded in assent. I knew it would do no good to protest. Anyway, every minute they spent here at the house gave Joel that much more chance of getting back safely—and honorably.

"Have you and your men eaten this morning?" I asked impulsively.

"Yes, ma'am. We ate on the road."

"Some hard bread, I suppose, and maybe a little cold meat?"

He nodded.

"I could fix you all some ham and eggs with bis-cuits and gravy in a short time. You can ride better with a hot meal under your belts." My heart was pounding so hard I was afraid he could see it. Those fierce eyes narrowed suspiciously, and I knew in dis-may that I had gone too far.

"Say, what is this? You tryin' to buy sympathy for that no-good deserter? It won't work, ma'am. He'll get what he. . . . Hey, wait a minute! He's not here! And he ain't been gone long!" He ran out the door. "He's makin' a break for it!" he shouted to the men. "Harve, Jesse—the creek! The rest of you come with me!"

He swung up into his saddle, then turned and touched his cap in a false salute. "Neat try, ma'am. Sorry it didn't work." He smiled a mocking half smile and turned the horse toward the woods, the men following.

"Wait! Please!" I begged, running to him and tak-ing hold of his stirrup. "You don't understand! He's on his way back. He's. . . ."

The captain kicked his stirrup free and spurred his horse. "He's no good, ma'am!" he called back as he ducked under the lowest green branches of the elms and locusts at the edge of the woods.

I stood in the yard, not knowing what to do for several precious seconds. Then I ran to the bell rope and swung on it with all my strength, hearing the loud iron clangs break the silence again and again. Joel would hear it if he were within earshot, as he surely would still be, and he would know I was warn-

ing him. Maybe he could take cover somewhere till the men had passed. He knew those woods like his own hands.

I heard an oath from one of the men. Then, as the bell sound died away, the silence was so deep I could hear my heart pounding in my ears. I stood leaning against the bell post. There was a buzzing in my head above that of the bees working in the blue morning glory vines that entwined the post. I shook my head to clear it, straining my ears in the heavy, heat-laden silence for any sound from the woods.

Finally it came, as deep down I had known it would. I heard a shout from up on the hill, then one sharp crack from a rifle that cut through my heart as if the bullet had found its mark there. I leaned my face against the rough, splintery wood of the post for a moment. In panic I gathered my long, full skirts above my knees and ran blindly toward the woods.

Ignoring the pain in my side and my burning lungs, I ran up the steep wooded slope, yanking my dress from the clutches of briars and underbrush, scarcely noticing the long, ragged cuts on my bare arms and legs.

He was dead. I knew it. Joel lay somewhere in these woods, his life pouring out onto the spongy carpet of past years' leaf mold. "Oh, God, help me to find him!" I sobbed as I ran. But there were no healing tears in my dry eyes and throbbing throat, only the bitter taste of despair. . . .

A blond giant of a man was running toward me

from the woods above. "What is it, sweetheart? What's wrong?"

Joel. . . . I must find Joel! *I veered to one side, but, in dismay, I felt his big hands catch hold of my sweater.*

My sweater? This was July. I wore no sweater. My arms below the puffed sleeves of the blue print were bare. . . .

I stopped in confusion. My arms were covered with the thick yellow knit of a sweater pulled down over a burr-studded short brown tweed skirt, wrinkled where I had clutched it in my attempt to keep my long skirts out from under my feet as I ran.

"Amanda! Answer me!" he demanded, shaking me a little. "What's happened?" . . .

. . . I stared at him blankly. Then, slowly, I began to recognize the loving concern in those deep blue eyes. *Tom! Oh, thank God! He isn't dead after all!* I took one stumbling step, and he caught me in his arms. The feel of them was comfortingly familiar. I held him so tightly my arms ached, and my salty tears blotted into his plaid hunting jacket.

"You're safe!" I babbled. "Oh, thank God, you're safe!"

"What's this all about? Of course, I'm safe. Are you all right?"

I nodded against his chest. I felt all right now that Tom was here, alive and not bleeding to death in the woods. But it wasn't Tom who lay bleeding! It was Joel! Joel?

Tom was smoothing my tangled hair and kissing my throbbing temples. "It's all right, baby. You must've heard my shot. You surely don't have much faith in my ability as a rifleman! Look, I got us a squirrel for supper. I told you I would."

He held up the furry gray body, lifeless now with a stain of blood on its head. So, the rifle shot was Tom killing the squirrel. . . .

. . . Joel might get back to camp after all. He was probably hiding somewhere in the woods. Maybe he would sneak back to tell me, but I hoped he wouldn't. No, it was best if he just rejoined his company and took whatever punishment his commander decided was right. Colonel Drummond was a just man, Joel said. . . .

. . . What was I thinking? Who was Joel? I was Amanda Farris. My husband, Tom, was holding me in his arms. I had no brown-haired, brown-eyed husband who was a deserter from the Union Army. The Union Army? The Civil War had been over for more than one hundred years! Surely all those who had fought in it were long since returned to dust. But what about those soldiers I'd talked with a few moments ago, who had drunk my water? They had worn blue Yankee uniforms, as Yankee as any I'd seen on TV or in the movies. Who were they? Who was the man I'd thought of as Joel?

A cold prickling fear went through my body, and then I knew. The man was Joel Harrison Adams, who lay buried under the stone tree stump with a squirrel on it. A small sob of fear escaped me, and Tom held me closer.

I carefully recalled the dreamlike events of the morning: Joel's leaving, putting on my long print dress, making the walnut bed with its patchwork quilt, then meeting the captain at the doorstep, carrying water from the spring in a wooden bucket, ringing the bell. I was supposed to have been doing a wash in my automatic washer with hot water drawn from our cistern and heated in an electric water heater in the kitchen. This was the 1980s, not the 1860s!

The autumn woods seemed oddly bare and lifeless after the green lushness of summer, as they had appeared a few moments ago. The air held a definite chill, but my shivering was not caused by the coolness of the weather.

Tom held me closer, trying to stop my trembling. His eyes reflected my horror as I clutched his jacket lapels with both hands.

"Help me, Tom!" I whimpered. "I think I'm going insane!"

E I G H T

Tom led me back to the house, but it was some time before I calmed down enough to tell him, as well as I could, what had happened.

"What can it all mean, Tom? The man in my kitchen, the soldiers, the children? And I know the names of all these people. It's . . . it's as though I'm watching scenes from a play out of the past, only I am one of the characters and I know all the lines!"

Am I going insane? Something inside me recoiled at the thought, but I had to face the possibility. "I have no way of knowing what hideous traits lie dormant in my genes!" I burst out. "For all I know, my family history may include Lizzie Borden, the Boston Strangler, and . . . and . . . the Mad Hatter!"

"Don't be ridiculous, Amanda!" Tom scolded, the expression on his face so horrified that I giggled. Then I began to cry.

He sat down in the rocking chair before the cold fireplace and held me on his lap, cuddling and comforting me as he would a child. I lay my aching head in the curve of his broad shoulder, feeling his love begin to fill the desolate hollows fear had made in my mind.

"It's just some passing thing, sweetheart," Tom said. "You've had some shock you didn't realize, or it's some temporary trauma caused by . . . oh, I don't know, maybe something simple like having your own home at last. You've wanted a family heritage so badly; maybe your subconscious is giving you one. Don't worry about it, sweetheart."

I could tell he was worried, nevertheless. Was he wondering what kind of monster he had married? Was he wondering about my unknown family now, too? I wished I hadn't brought up the subject. I didn't want his pity.

Suddenly a new thought hit me: *Would Tom love me if he seriously thought I was going insane?* I fought off the smothering panic the thought unleashed. I had to have his love to survive!

I vowed I wouldn't let Tom see me in any more of these "spells." If the hallucinations, or whatever they were, persisted, I simply would fight them off. Surely my need for Tom's love was strong enough to enable me to combat any threat to it. And surely his presence in the house all weekend would keep the "spells" at bay.

A sinus headache haunted me for the rest of the weekend, draining me of energy, but I bubbled with enthusiasm for all Tom's suggestions. Determined to seem my normal self, but mostly to avoid being alone, I even accompanied him to church in Lexington both Sunday morning and Sunday night.

Both Saturday and Sunday nights I went to bed with Tom before eleven o'clock, not wanting to be up alone, as I often was, working on some project or reading a good book. The extra rest didn't seem to do me any good, though.

When Tom left for work Monday morning, I went through my chores listlessly. Finally, after lunch, I gave in to my headache and lethargy and stretched out across the bed.

I must have dozed off, for I was awakened by huge shudders that went all the way from my head to my feet, almost like convulsions. I was resisting something with all my strength, and gradually I became aware that I was repeating, "No! No! You can't!" With one final convulsive shudder, I relaxed on the bed, limp and sweating, but free of whatever it was I had been fighting.

Was it simply a nightmare? I wondered, lying there feeling waves of relief at its absence. *Surely it was only a dream!* Or was my subconscious aware of some spiritual struggle of which my conscious mind knew nothing? Could it be possible that from the first time I'd seen that gray house, I had been under some spirit's influence?

Stated flatly, it sounded ridiculous. I didn't even believe such things were possible. But then I didn't really believe pictures could be sent through the air and arrive intact in my living room via a TV set, and yet I sat before the TV many nights enthralled by some story.

Now that I thought about it, several of my recent experiences equalled anything I had ever seen on any of the TV shows that specialized in the macabre. According to the writers and hosts of these shows, many things are astir in the world of which we ordinary mortals have no inkling as we go about our everyday lives, unless some bizarre circumstance causes the physical world and the spiritual world to coincide. Could it be that my mind was not playing tricks, after all, but that my usual world had coincided with some spirit that was abroad in this secluded valley, as both Chad and Mr. Roberts had tried to convince me?

I couldn't quite accept that, but all at once I wanted to know more about this place and the tragedies that Mr. Roberts claimed had caused a curse to be put on it.

For several minutes longer, I lay there drained by my nightmarish battle. At the same time, I felt strangely buoyed by the conviction that I was sane, as sane as Tom, and was merely caught up in some supernatural experience.

I didn't wonder then why I, and not Tom, had gotten involved in all this. I began to look forward with excitement to the next revelation, and I resolved to learn all I could about my predecessors here on Deserter's Creek. The name itself was intriguing in the light of my experiences with the Union Army on Saturday morning.

Perhaps, in some unfathomable way, my mind was like a recorder playing back scenes from the past which, somehow, were still in the atmosphere around my new home. This didn't explain my recent battle with someone or something, but I was feeling better now, my energy coming back as I arose and began to dress. I had a new confidence in my ability to cope with whatever might happen here.

I coiled my hair neatly, slipped on my "sensible" light gray wool suit, and tucked a dark green scarf at my throat for an ascot. I stepped into green suede heels, grabbed gray gloves and a green suede purse, and went to the full-length mirror on the bathroom door to see if I looked my sanest. I wanted no room for doubt. Satisfied with the image that smiled back at me, I located Annabel's keys and went out.

Black Night ran up to accept his usual adoration, but he had to settle for a wave and some baby talk. He watched resignedly from the end of the walk as I drove off.

About halfway between our place and the church, I overtook Chad wearing his faded, ragged jeans and a shrunken sweater. He was carrying a large peanut butter jar filled with bright-colored leaves. I stopped the car and leaned across the seat to open the door for him.

"On your way to the graveyard?" I asked.

He nodded, concentrating on the jar so that no water would spill as he climbed in beside me.

I pointed to the beautiful spray of scarlet leaves he had mixed in with some orange maple leaves. "What gorgeous color!" I exclaimed, touching a cluster of white berries. "What are they?"

"Poison ivy."

Hastily, I drew back my pointing finger. "Aren't you afraid you'll break out with blisters and swell up and itch?"

"Naw." That seemed to be the end of that topic of conversation, so I searched for another as we drove along.

"I just love autumn," I said, waving my left hand

toward the trees that lined Deserter's Creek Road on either side. "The crisp air, the pretty colors of the leaves, the—"

"I don't!" Chad broke in vehemently. "Them leaves are dead!"

And there's another topic likewise, I thought. We rode in silence to the graveyard fence. I stopped Annabel, and Chad climbed out as carefully as he had climbed in. Without a thank you, or a good-bye, or even a "kiss-my-foot," he was gone. I looked back in the rearview mirror as I drove on and saw him trudging around the corner of the church, clutching his jar of poison ivy and maple leaves.

What a weird kid! I thought as I drove into town. He seemed so old and worldly-wise for his years. How I longed to give him the childhood he seemed to have missed! But I put such thoughts behind me as the courthouse came into view.

Mr. Roberts was out for the afternoon, so I wrote him a short note, renewing my invitation for supper and tentatively setting the date for the coming Friday night. "Call me if you can't make it Friday, and we will make other arrangements," I concluded. I added my new phone number at the bottom, signed it, and extracted a promise from Janie that she would see that Mr. Roberts got it as soon as he came in.

I was disappointed at not being able to ask Mr. Roberts about the history of our place, but I consoled myself with thoughts of Friday night.

Suddenly I thought of going to the library to look up back copies of any newspaper that might have been published in the town during the 1860's. I found the narrow brick building easily, but the friendly, middle-aged librarian told me there had been no newspaper in the small town then. She suggested I take out a library card anyway and became even friendlier when she found out who I was.

"I remember Tom well!" she said warmly. "He was continually after books on famous trials. He started out with Perry Mason and ended up with F. Lee Bailey," she said with a laugh. "Did he become a lawyer, as he always planned? He was going to be a famous criminal lawyer, I believe."

I laughed with her. "He's a lawyer, but I don't think F. Lee Bailey is too worried yet," I answered, telling her about Tom's plans to set up a local practice. I thought she'd never stop talking after that, but finally I was able to make an exit, carrying four books on ghosts, possession, spiritual phenomena, and a couple of novels I grabbed so she wouldn't think I was a fanatic on the supernatural.

From the library, I went to the supermarket across from the courthouse and picked up some things for Friday's supper. I did odds-and-ends shopping at the dime store. At both places, my status as a stranger in town went unchallenged.

Then I decided to visit the drugstore, more to familiarize myself with the town than because I needed anything.

The druggist looked me over boldly as I walked into the store, then smiled. "Tourist or new resident?" he asked over his shoulder as he located the brand of aspirin I had requested.

I smiled back at him. If I hadn't been married, I probably would have spent a lot of time in that drugstore. He was in his late twenties or early thirties, with black hair and possibly the blackest eyes I'd ever seen.

"New resident," I answered. "Amanda Farris. *Mrs!*"

He made a face. "Mrs. Who?"

"Thomas Farris. We've built a home out on Deserter's Creek Road. My husband's—"

"Captain of the basketball squad," he finished for me. "Class of '72! You say you've moved here? Man, I can't wait to see old Tom! He hasn't been back that I know of since his grandparents died soon after he went away to college, and I completely lost track of him. He was gonna be a big criminal lawyer, I remember. Did he make it?"

"Well, he's a lawyer with a big firm in Lexington, but he's planning to open a practice here in town as soon as he can find an office."

"Hey, you're serious!" He handed me my change and leaned his elbows on the counter. "Would you answer a question for me, doll?"

I nodded, a bit flustered by his approach.

"Why?"

"Why, what?" I repeated.

"Who, when, where, and how," he finished, laughing. "The elements of any good newspaper story." He bowed as low as the counter permitted. "Daren Blake, editor of the school paper, class of '73. No, I mean why is old Tom comin' back here? This town has been dead so long it doesn't even smell bad anymore. It's just a clean white skeleton that nobody ever took the trouble to bury. If it weren't for Dad, I'd be as far away from here as. . . ." He reached into his pocket, pulled out some change, and counted it. ". . . As $1.42 would take me!" he said with a laugh.

His good humor was infectious, and I joined his laughter. "Tom wants a small-town practice like his granddad had here. Nostalgia, partly, I guess, and since you know him, I suppose you know about Tom's weakness for people?"

He nodded. "Still the same old Good Samaritan, huh?"

"That's Tom exactly," I agreed eagerly. "And he enjoys every minute of it."

"Yeah. Tom always was religious. Oh, not a sober-sided, long-faced religious. He was great fun, but he always had some sort of deep commitment, you know? Sort of a God-and-fellowman thing. I remember he missed most of the senior prom because he stopped to help some guy with car trouble—in his rented tux! He ended up taking the guy all the way to Louis-ville so he wouldn't miss his kid's birthday party. Or so the guy told Tom. I'd bet dollars to donuts he was meetin' some broad, but old Tom never could resist a sob story."

"Amen!" I said fervently.

Daren grinned. "I remember Tom almost married Karen Haynes because she was pregnant and nobody else would. It took the whole basketball team and me to talk him out of it. Tom never had been out with Karen, you understand. He didn't go much for that kind of girl. He and Eleanor Hobson had some-thing pretty serious going for a while, though, until the prom thing. She never forgave him. But he just felt sorry for Karen."

"That's Tom, all right," I agreed, hiding the pang of jealousy I felt over Eleanor Hobson. I had never asked Tom about his past loves, and he never talked about them. "What happened to her?" I asked, then wished I hadn't. But Daren misunderstood my question.

"Karen? Oh, she went away somewhere, and we kept our star basketball player. But it was a close one!" He stood there a moment, obviously reminiscing. Then he came back to the present with that infectious, crooked smile.

"Tell old Tom to get down here to see me as soon as he can. Man, it'll be great to have him back!"

"I'll tell him," I promised as I turned to leave.

I was going out the door when he gave that age-old wolf whistle. But it was such a friendly whistle that I couldn't help acknowledging it with a wave and a smile.

NINE

My foray into our new town and my encounter with Daren Blake had given me new enthusiasm. My lethargy was gone completely now, and I found that I was enjoying the drive home along our winding country road.

Frost and wind had thinned the leaves. Only the deep red oaks and a few orange maples added color to the bare walnuts and sycamores. Occasionally I caught sight of a bright red ivy vine with white berries that twined its rough stem around a dark trunk.

I briefly stopped the car at the edge of the road and got out to pluck a handful of wild grapes. I enjoyed their tart taste as I resumed driving, this time with the window down, so I could dispose of the seeds.

The road wound endlessly, it seemed, through a smoky blue haze that held picturesque golden haystacks and leaning gray barns, one with the scarlet leaves of trumpet vines climbing to its rusting crown. The whole road seemed especially created for visual pleasure. There were only a few beer or soft drink cans and one ugly dumping spot along the creek bank. But then, there were only half a dozen or so houses on this road, including ours.

I passed the leaning, rusty mailbox before I saw the faded name: PALMER. I braked and backed Annabel to the end of the rocky lane beside the box, convinced the lane led to Chad's home. I'd never noticed the mailbox before, possibly because it had never been free of horseweeds until the frost had cut them.

The house was not visible from the lane. Suddenly I had the urge to see where Chad lived, to meet his mother. *Maybe I can invite her over for coffee some morning,* I planned as I drove carefully up the rutted lane. *Or I can ask for Chad's help with some chore.* His neglected appearance had already prejudiced me against Mrs. Palmer, but perhaps my prejudice was unfair. For all I knew, she could be an overworked, overburdened woman trying to provide the necessities for a large family and too worn out to care about anything else.

Chad wasn't dirty just by accident, though. He had been working on it without interference for some time now. I couldn't help feeling that basic cleanliness was a necessity, regardless of the ragged clothing he wore. Surely in this country at this time, anyone who wanted to could afford soap! Still, for the boy's sake, I made up my mind to be agreeable to Mrs. Palmer. I wanted to help him if I could.

I had to laugh at my do-good plans as I guided Annabel around still another deep rut in the seemingly unending lane. *If I'm not careful, I'll be just like Tom!* I thought.

The house came into view—a narrow, unpainted wooden building with a rusted tin roof, a covered porch at the front, and soot-blackened spots under the windows that gave it the weary look of a woman with dark circles under her eyes. It sat on a small rise at the side of the lane, which bumped on toward a small dilapidated barn.

As I parked Annabel and got out, I heard a door slam around back and caught a glimpse of a running figure that disappeared around the barn before I could decide if it had been Chad or some other boy about his size.

I saw the torn lace curtain at the front window move as I mounted the two sagging steps to the porch. The door opened at my first knock.

"Mrs. Palmer?" I asked, with a smile that I felt sure did not quite cover my dismay.

She nodded shortly, her faded blue eyes wary.

"I'm Amanda Farris," I plunged in before I could change my mind and leave. "I just—"

"I know who ya are," Mrs. Palmer interrupted. "What do ya want?"

I gasped, feeling as if I had been slapped. "Why, I . . . ah . . . wondered if Chad could . . . help me with some . . . leaf-raking," I stammered. There weren't really any leaves in my new yard. The trees we had planted would be no problem for some time, and the older trees were too far from the house to drop leaves in the yard. But I had been planning to start a compost heap, and faced with her belligerence, I couldn't think of a better excuse.

I certainly didn't want Mrs. Palmer's company for coffee! I didn't think I could eat or drink in her presence. She was as dirty as Chad, perhaps more so, for her face held caked makeup, blush, and eye shadow that hadn't been completely removed for quite awhile. Her strawlike hair hung about her shoulders, and I shuddered to think how long it might have been since it had been washed.

As she tightened the belt of her grimy blue nylon quilted robe, I caught a whiff of a heavy perfume that didn't quite cover other less-pleasant odors. *I definitely don't want to make a bosom pal of Mrs. Palmer!* I thought. But I did want to help Chad.

I swallowed my revulsion and smiled at her in what I hoped was a winning way. "I owe Chad for helping me the other day," I said with sudden inspiration.

She opened the door and held it for me. "Come in," she invited, with a smile that revealed yellowed teeth.

From the porch, I hadn't been able to see inside the dim room. Once inside, I found myself in a fairly large space—not quite living room and not quite bedroom, for it obviously served as both. A wide white iron bed with chipped paint and rumpled covers filled one back corner of the room across from an enclosed stairway with the two bottom steps spilling out below the closed door. The floor was covered with blue-flowered linoleum whose pattern had been worn away in spots, but not from cleaning. Down a step at the back, I glimpsed a narrow kitchen with a water pump at the sink under the back window.

Mrs. Palmer moved some clothes from the corner of a sagging couch and motioned me to a seat. She crossed over to a front corner to turn down the TV, leaving the bright-colored images flashing on the small screen.

I passed up the faded blue plush sofa and perched on the edge of a straight wooden chair, growing angrier by the minute at the warped sense of values that placed color TV higher on a list of priorities than a child's clothes and self-respect.

She went to the kitchen and shouted out the back door for Chad. I was beginning to understand why he had run when he had seen me coming. I was feeling embarrassed for him and wishing I hadn't come, when he came in.

At the sight of me, he broke off the tune he was whistling as though he hadn't known I was there. I had to admire his nerve and his acting ability, but maybe he was unaware that I had seen him when I'd driven up.

"Old lady run you off?" he asked, flicking me an impish, sideways grin.

I laughed. "Not yet!"

"You watch your tongue, boy!" Mrs. Palmer snapped at Chad. "You know what that. . . ." She threw me a quick, wary glance. "You know what she did to your papa," she finished mildly, giving me an apologetic look. "It don't pay to speak evil of the dead," she added in a pious tone.

I ignored her. "Chad, I didn't pay you for your work the other day in the graveyard, and you've not been back since. How much do I owe you?"

It was the first time I had ever seen him lose composure. His face was flushed as he crossed to the TV, switched channels, and turned up the sound.

"Chad!" His mother came swiftly into the room from the kitchen doorway. "You mind your manners! The lady here asked you a question. You show a little respect, now!"

He tossed long hair out of smoldery dark eyes. "You don't owe me nothin'," he muttered.

"Oh, yes, I do!" I said firmly, feeling like an overzealous elephant in a watermelon patch. "You worked a good three hours for me that day and furnished the tools as well."

Chad shook his head stubbornly, his eyes on the flashing TV screen.

"Chad!" his mother scolded. "Don't pay him no mind, ma'am. He's just like his old man, stubborn as a mule and twice as nasty tempered when he takes a notion."

I laughed uncertainly. "That's all right." I reached into my purse and took out a ten-dollar bill. Out of the corner of my eye, I saw Chad's mother twisting her hands together, while Chad studiously ignored me.

Suddenly I felt ashamed of myself. I got up, stuck the money in her hands, mumbled something about her taking it for him, and left.

All the way back down the lane, I berated myself for having barged into Chad's home life. I might never see him again, and there was so much I wanted to do for him.

By the time I reached home, I felt confused and depressed—the proper state of mind for Lucretia.

TEN

The house itself seemed full of grief as I opened the door and stepped from the bright autumn day into the comparative gloom of the foyer. An oppressive sadness and despair weighted my spirit and pounded dully at my temples and the top of my head.

I shivered as I passed quickly through the foyer and into the kitchen where I set my packages on the table. I felt an aching desire to cry, but I had no tears. I was limp and exhausted with grief that, instead of spilling out in a cleansing tide of tears, turned inward. A strange bitterness was shriveling me like a blighted apple that turns dark and twisted under the same sun and rain that causes its fellows to thrive. . . .

. . . Isn't my life already blighted? *I asked myself. What was there left for me now that Joel lay in there white and still, shot down like a mad dog when he was on his way back? What hurt so much, aside from losing him, was the fact that all my protests were* met with hidden smiles and nodding heads in the almost universal belief that I was excusing Joel now that he was dead.

What a final, hopeless word—dead. Never again would those long, gentle fingers, now so unnaturally still, caress my hair or my cheek. Never would they coax a fiddle to sing or carve pretties out of wood for the children. Never again would I feel that strong arm protectively around my shoulders or lovingly around my waist. Nor would I hold that head of unruly hair in my lap, soothing him as I would one of the children. I would never again feel the scratch of his beard or the safe, warm feeling of my head fitting like part of a puzzle into the hollow of that lean shoulder.

Grief rose within me like gall. I could feel nausea rising in my stomach with every breath of lily-scented air and the ache of unshed tears in my throbbing head. But my eyes were as dry and hollow as holes burned in a piece of wood. I knew it without looking in a mirror. In the morning, as I was pinning up my hair, they had stared back at me like stranger's eyes in a stranger's pale, wooden face.

I was made of wood outside. Inside I ached as no wood surely ever ached!

I didn't care how I looked. I'd dressed with such care only because of Joel. He was here in the parlor, even though those poor closed eyes could not see me. He was here and our neighbors were here and I would not shame him before them.

If only they would all go and leave Joel and me alone these last precious moments! But some of them stuck to me like burrs at every turn, trying to force *gifts of food down my wooden throat. Didn't they know it only hung there in a lump and would not go down? I had to force myself to swallow the scalding tea they thrust at me. If only they would let me alone! I knew they meant well, but I couldn't say a proper good-bye to Joel with all those greedy eyes upon me.*

Please, please make them go! Just for an hour! That's all I ask. Please, God, make them leave us alone awhile! They'll put him in the churchyard tomorrow, and I won't have had a moment alone with him.

"Oh, Joel, Joel, I can't bear them putting you in the ground! Joel! Joel! Oh, no, no, no . . . !" The screaming seemed to come from somewhere outside me, but it tore my throat as it poured out.

Concerned hands reached out, but I evaded them and pushed my way to the cedar box on the trestles in the parlor, that box that held my life. I studied the dear face, memorizing, storing it in memory against the empty days ahead. Hard, dry, racking sobs shook my body, but still without the relief of tears. I reached out and touched his face. It was cold and unresponsive—Joel, who had been so warm, so alive, so in love with all life that it had made him physically ill to kill a chicken for dinner. I fell to my knees beside the box, feeling his presence there, speaking to him alone.

"They won't believe me, Joel, that you were goin' back. They brand you deserter. But we know, sweetheart, you and I. And God knows how you hated killing. You're a good man, Joel, a gentle man, and. . . . Oh, Joel, I love you!"

I screamed as they tried to drag me away, pulling my arms and shoulders, clucking and soothing with false, comforting words. I shook them off.

"Leave us alone! All of you! Oh, God, please make them leave us alone!"

They fell back then, their resentment thick around me, but I cared nothing for that. They had driven Joel's spirit away from me, and my emptiness was unbearable.

"Joel, don't leave me!" I begged. "Oh, God, I can't stand it! Let him stay with me! Give him back to me—"

"Mrs. Adams." It was the minister's voice. "Mrs. Adams, Joel's body is dead, but his spirit has gone to . . . to God." I had caught the hesitation. He wasn't sure because of Joel's desertion. But what had that to do with his relationship to God? Joel had loved God and had respected life so much he could not snuff it out like an unwanted candle flame, as so many of the men here did for pleasure when they hunted. As the soldiers had done to Joel. Did that deny him heaven? If so, I didn't want any part of it either, and I told them so.

I could see it in their faces, even in the face of the minister. They still believed Joel had shot himself, believed the captain's lie that Joel had grabbed the rifle out of his hands and had shot himself to keep from going back.

"It was a lie!" I screamed at them. Joel would never have taken his own life or anyone else's. The captain was a fanatic who had shot Joel without trial and then had lied to protect himself.

"Mrs. Adams, you must pull yourself together for the sake of the children."

My head snapped up at the minister's words. I had forgotten the children! If anything happened to them—to Tarrellton. . . . They were all I had now.

"If God has any mercy in him, which I'm beginning to doubt," I told them deliberately, "he won't separate any of us again."

The minister gasped. "Mrs. Adams, you don't know what you're saying!"

I ignored him. "As these people are my witnesses, God, I beg you not to part us one by one. Take us all together next time!" It wasn't so much a prayer as a desperate refusal to go through this anguish again.

I jumped up before they could stop me and ran outside. Joel's spirit had to be out here somewhere in this hot July morning, and I intended to find it again, to keep it near me until I could join him.

The sun beat down upon me, but I felt I could never be warm again. The dog looked up eagerly and started toward me. I put out my hand toward him. He stopped and sniffed the air. His dark eyes rolled in fear, and his tail sought the safety of his stomach.

"Come, boy," I coaxed. I couldn't seem to think of his name. He backed off, his eyes rolling sideways at me. The primeval sound of his howling sent shivers down my spine. "Are you cryin' for him, too, boy?" I choked, ready to cry. Still no tears came. What I suffered was too deep for tears.

The dog turned and ran. I heard him hit the back of his house as he threw himself inside. The house *trembled with moans that came from deep within.*

They had me then—all the shocked, good people —making me swallow scalding tea dosed with foul-tasting powder, almost as vile as their service to me while they despised Joel. I slept a dull, drugged sleep beneath the patchwork quilt in the walnut bed. . . .

. . . Tom was home. I heard the car door slam as I jumped up guiltily from the bed and straightened the blue and yellow spread. How long had I slept here when I should have been getting supper? *I'm getting strangely lazy,* I thought. I had always been so full of energy.

I rushed into the kitchen and stopped in bewilderment. The frozen vegetables I had bought for Friday night's supper sat soggy in their plastic bags. Why hadn't I put them away? I would have to use the thawed food right away and shop again for Friday. What had come over me that I would lie down and sleep the afternoon away without a thought for perishable food?

I began opening the thawed packages and dumping vegetables into pans for cooking. The steaks were cool, but definitely thawed. I put two on to cook and put the other in a pan for Black Night. He would have a special treat tonight.

Then it all came flooding back—the dog's fear, the people, the despair. I grabbed the table edge for support as it bore down on me again. And in spite of the fact that I had awakened in bed, I knew this time that I hadn't dreamed it. It was another of those unexplainable scenes from the past that kept haunting me. Black Night's strange fear had something to do with whatever it was that took my mind over so completely.

If she can take over my mind this way, I thought fearfully, *can she take me over entirely until I become Lucretia?* And what then of myself, Amanda? Would I wander this valley, lost and searching for a body, as Lucretia apparently had done for more than a hundred years? Or would I simply cease to exist, smothered out by a stronger personality?

I heard Tom's steps on the walk and ran to straighten my mussed hair and change my rumpled clothes. I must not tell him I had experienced another of these . . . whatever they were. I couldn't risk it. Yet I needed someone with whom I could talk, someone who could advise me. A psychiatrist, perhaps, or a minister.

I pictured polite, proper Reverend Lawson at First Church in Lexington and suppressed a giggle at the thought of the horror that would spread across his dignified face at such a tale. He would shun me like the plague, convinced I was either a crackpot or on drugs. Tom would never forgive me!

I knew no other minister well, and seeing a psychiatrist seemed such an admission of mental instability. Yet I was more and more convinced that my mind wasn't playing tricks, that something beyond what most of us ever experience or even suspect was happening here.

Tom came in, and I greeted him in my usual way. As we chatted through supper, Tom remarked jokingly about the variety of food I served him, and I told him of my encounter with Daren Blake. Then, remembering Eleanor Hobson, I had a sudden desire to nudge Tom's jealousy a little.

"He's very attractive, Tom. Wonder why he hasn't married?"

"Dare?" Tom laughed. "He's been married ever since he finished high school. He married the girl he went steady with all through high school, and she helped put him through college. He adores her. The last I heard, they had four kids."

"But he. . . ."

"Yeah, I know. He flirted with you and told you how dead our town is. Dare's a big talker, was going to be a newspaper reporter in New York or somewhere, but he studied pharmacy and went in partners with his dad, just as we all knew he would."

Daren had made me feel so attractive, too! My ego slightly deflated, I slipped out after supper to give Black Night his steak. I put the meat in his dish and stooped down beside it, waiting to see if he still feared me. "If you turn me down, Black Night," I told him, "it will just about finish me!" But he sniffed the air, watched me cautiously for a second, then came eagerly to me. He let me pat and scratch him while he ate. It was hard to believe he had howled at the sight of me this afternoon.

Could I have dreamed the whole thing? I wondered doubtfully. The coffin, the people, the dog's fright? If so, my dreams were running in a logical sequence, for the man in the coffin was the man in my kitchen that first Sunday when this whole nightmare began. And his death fit my experience of the day the soldiers came.

What next? I pondered. "Tune in tomorrow, same

time, same station," I intoned dramatically, "for the next episode in the life of Lucretia Adams." And, in spite of my fear, I felt a shiver of anticipation. I had become so interested in her story, I no longer was sure I wanted the scenes to stop. So far, Lucretia had left me alone when Tom was around, and this convinced me I could let her show me the rest of her story and be brought safely back to reality when Tom came in.

Like an alcoholic housewife who drinks the cooking sherry in the daytime, thinking she can hide the fact from her husband, I was hooked on my psychic experiences. And I gravely underestimated Lucretia, or whatever it was.

ELEVEN

Tuesday passed uneventfully. Wednesday morning Mr. Roberts called. " 'The turnpike road to most people's hearts, I find,' " he quoted, " 'lies through their mouths, or I mistake mankind.' Woolcott was right, little lady, and I'm no exception. I'll be there Friday with bells on!"

Tom called at noon. "Hey, Manda, guess who was in the office just now! Daren Blake. It was great to see him! I'd almost forgotten how likable he really is. Uh, sweetheart, do you think you could manage a couple more for supper Friday night?"

"You've already asked him to supper." It wasn't a question. "OK, who's the other guy?"

"Not another guy, sweetheart," he corrected. "Daren's wife, Lisa. You'll like her. You have a lot in common—"

"OK, Tom," I interrupted. "Cut the soft sell. It's all right."

"I love you," he said. Then he gave me Lisa Blake's

number so I could call and make the invitation official. I was smiling when I hung up the phone. That was typical Tom, but it was time I met some of these old friends of his.

The house didn't need cleaning, but I went over it anyway. The rest of the morning I spent cleaning the upstairs windows, using a razor blade to scrape off the paper labels left on them ever since the house had been completed. We didn't use the upstairs, and I just never had gotten around to this job.

The upstairs had only a floor and four walls with a roof over them. The house was a story-and-a-half design, a Cape Cod three-quarter house, Eric Dunaway had called it. I had wanted the upper story simply because my visionary gray house had required one, but when Tom and I had our family, we could put in extra bedrooms up here under the sloping eaves.

At noon, I stopped for a bowl of canned tomato soup and a grilled cheese sandwich. I had worked steadily all morning, and as I sat over my second cup of hot tea, I felt the pleasant tiredness that comes from hard physical labor that has produced satisfying results.

I remembered one of the girls at work complaining that she hated moving into a new house because it was all there, complete. She didn't feel at home until the newness had worn off and she didn't have to feel guilty every time she drove a nail into the unblemished walls.

I didn't feel that way about my house. I had been at home from that first day I'd seen the mystical gray house shimmering in the summer sun. I loved every plank and nail in our home with a passion nearly equal to the way I loved Tom. Nothing about keeping my house was a chore. Waxing the floors and woodwork, polishing the windows, even scrubbing the hearthstones—each stroke was a caress. And the house seemed to respond with a special glow.

Did Lucretia feel this way about the weathered gray house that was the "ancestor" of my new home? The thought itself was an invitation, and I knew it. But I had come so far in my knowledge of her history, it was like reading new chapters of an engrossing story. I was alone. I wouldn't worry Tom with it. When he came in, though, I would be safe again. Perhaps by being the instigator rather than a victim, I would be able to control the visit.

I haven't seen her anymore as I did on the creek bank and in the garden, I mused. Could this be because, now that she was taking over my thoughts so completely, when I entered into those scenes from the past, I was Lucretia? Would it now be impossible for me to see her without looking into a mirror?

Don't be ridiculous! I told myself. *She doesn't "take me over." She merely shows me her story, like a TV rerun.*

This time I felt her presence before my thoughts were hers. I sensed no feeling of cold, no musky gravelike odor, as some of the ghost stories I had brought from the library suggested. The sunlight streaming through the polished window into the kitchen simply dimmed a little. The cheerful copper-bottomed pots and pans hanging over my stove seemed alien in the gloom and finally faded altogether.

The kitchen was mine, and yet it was not. There

was a stone fireplace where my electric range had stood, with iron pots and utensils hanging from iron hooks around it. The thick wooden table and ladder-back chairs were much like mine.

My lethargy increased. Thick, oppressive grief pressed in on me like a weight, suffocating me, making me want to cry; and yet I seemed to know that this grief went deeper than tears—a dense, dark despair so heavy within me that it would hold my spirit forever imprisoned in that dead emptiness that replaced pain, that went beyond feeling. I could feel my consciousness blending into hers. . . .

. . . The fire was burning low, but I planned not to replenish it until just before the children came in from school. The wood the boys and I had cut was too precious to waste. There were plenty of coals to finish baking the potatoes I had buried in the ashes. I wished I had something better to offer them, but even without butter, potatoes were nourishing and would fill their stomachs with warmth after their long, cold walk.

There had been another scene with Tarrellton this morning! His coat sleeves were too short and he had tried to slip out without it. But the ground had been white with frost and the November wind had blown cold. When I had insisted he wear the coat, that sullen look had closed over his face.

"I'm sorry, baby," I had said, putting my arms around him. "I just can't get you a new coat right now. Maybe. . . ."

He had jerked free. "I ain't askin' for a new coat! I just ain't cold, that's all!"

I had made him wear it, though, knowing all the

while that I was adding one more scar to those he already bore.

He needed new books, too. Already he had gone through Harrison's old ones twice. For that matter, Harrison needed new ones, too. He knew my old arithmetic backwards and forwards and could recite my reader from memory. But Harrison didn't mind that. His schoolwork was easy this way, and he could have more time with his grandfather on the farm.

Susannah was just beginning to read in the primer the boys had used. She was content with her life at school. At home, she missed her father, but she was asking for him less now. And she was becoming protective of the rest of us, worrying over any of us who felt ill, especially her idol, Tarrellton.

I could understand her feelings. How I longed to get Tarrellton the things he needed—new clothes for his dignity and that blue-backed U.S. history book he wanted so badly. Tarrellton had the makings of a great man. I could sense it. If only I could keep that unique spirit alive! He never would be satisfied to settle down on the farm. He was like my father, Dr. Amos Tarrellton, for whom he was named. He had ambition, drive. . . .

The front door slammed, and I jumped up to throw a log on the fire, watching it blaze up in sparks of blue, red, and yellow.

The children came in, their faces reddened from the cold. Tarrellton's lip was bleeding, and he was in his shirt sleeves, the hated coat slung across one shoulder. His shirt was filthy.

"It got the sleeve torn out, Ma," he said, avoiding my eyes as he held out the coat.

I felt a current of anger run through me. "You hated that coat, Tarrellton!" I screamed at him. "You deliberately destroyed it!"

Frantic with worry about how I could replace it, I wouldn't listen to any of their protests that he had been in a fight.

"He hit Coley Fraley 'cause he said Daddy was a coward, Mama!" Susannah babbled. "And Coley grabbed—"

"Shut up, Susannah!" Tarrellton snarled. "I don't care what you think!" he shouted back at me, an ugly snarl on his lips. I slapped his face hard.

I gasped as the shock of the blow ran up my arm. Three pairs of eyes stared up at me—Susannah's, wide and tearful; Harrison's, puzzled and embarrassed; and Tarrellton's. . . . Would I ever forget the bitter look in those dark eyes that once had been so alight with some inner glow? Now, except for brief flares of hatred, they were a dull, flat black like the extinguished wick of a candle.

I sank down on the hearth and covered my face with my hands. A hopeless, empty sobbing tore through my body and out of my throat with a dreadful wrenching sound that had Susannah crying wildly and Harrison running from one of us to the other with soothing hands and words. The front door slammed behind Tarrellton.

He'll never get over that slap, *I thought achingly.* To think I'd let my despair vent itself on this beloved child, already so scarred by the turn our lives had taken!

Harrison led Susannah out of the room, and I could hear him telling her a story.

"Oh, Joel," I sobbed, alone in the kitchen. "I need you so much! If you are alive somewhere, please come to me! If it's only your spirit, Joel, if I just could know you were there! Please come to me! Help me!"

"Amanda, what's wrong?"

A thrill of happiness surged through me as his arms closed around me and lifted me from the hearth. "Oh, Joel, you're here!"

The blond head jerked back as though I'd slapped him, too. This wasn't Joel! The muscular arms of a tall stranger held me imprisoned. I screamed, pushing at him, struggling to be free of his hateful embrace, sobbing hysterically until the sting of his slap brought me up short.

"Amanda, what is this?" he demanded, holding me at arm's length, his blue eyes searching mine in disbelief. Suddenly I went limp, fighting darkness, and felt his arms catch me before I could fall. . . .

. . . It was over quickly. I was Amanda Farris and I was in my husband's arms. My tears fell silently, blotting into his shirt.

Tom raised my head, forcing me to look at him, and I saw that his eyes held fear. "If you know what's going on, for God's sake tell me!" he begged. "If you don't, then you've got to get help, see a doctor. . . ."

I tried to explain, but as I talked, I could see the fear growing in him.

"You think I'm crazy, don't you?" I said finally. "You don't believe a word I've been saying." I turned away from the frank admission in his eyes.

"It's not that I don't believe you. I believe you're telling me the truth as you see it. But, Amanda, think how it all sounds! A spirit has roamed this valley for over a hundred years, lures you here, influences you to rebuild her house, and finally tries to take over your body? It's incredible! Totally fantastic!"

I was too tired to argue and still very much absorbed by Lucretia's problems. My sympathy for the little family in their desperate need was as real as though it were all happening to a friend here and now. In a way it was worse, for there was absolutely no way I could cross the time barrier to help them. Whatever had been the outcome of their tragic lives, it was too late for me to do anything about it. Yet, the hungry children in their outgrown clothing, bewildered by their mother's despair, haunted me as much now that Lucretia was gone as they had when I had been seeing them through her eyes. How I longed to be able to ease their burdens somehow!

"Tom, why didn't God help Lucretia Adams? Does he enjoy seeing people suffer?"

"Sweetheart, God has promised never to forsake his children. If this Lucretia Adams had belonged to God, he would have given her the strength to face her troubles, and he would have helped her."

"But, Tom, I don't understand. You're always telling people that we are all God's children."

"We are all God's children in the sense that he made us all, but to really know him, we have to make a conscious choice and invite him to be a part of our lives. He doesn't force himself on anyone, but only those who choose to know him have any right to call upon him for help."

"I don't understand," I repeated. "Why do we have

to 'choose to know him'? Why aren't we all automatically . . . ?"

Tom was shaking his head. "God does not want us
to love him because we are blind, obedient robots
programmed to love our Creator. He wants us to love
him by choice."

"Isn't that sort of like a communist election?" I
asked sarcastically. "Only one name on the ballot?"

"Oh, there's always Satan, Amanda. Some people
choose to follow him."

"Tom!" I gasped. "I'm sure Lucretia didn't do that!"

"Maybe not, but many people think they can just
blunder through life without making any choice at
all. Lucretia Adams may have been one of those."

"But why did God send such evil on her? She really
wasn't a bad person—"

"Sweetheart, God is love. He doesn't send evil on
people. Matthew says, 'He makes his sun to rise on
the evil and on the good, and sends rain on the just
and on the unjust.' When evil things happen to
people, those who know God are given the strength
and protection they need to overcome them."

"Then why does he allow evil to happen, Tom?
Doesn't he have the power to stop it? I think he just
doesn't care," I babbled on. "He allowed his own Son
to die horribly and he—"

"Amanda!" Tom's shocked voice cut into the bitter
tirade that I suddenly wasn't sure belonged entirely
to me. "Don't you realize that watching someone you
love suffer hurts more than going through it yourself?"

I pushed aside the memory of Lucretia's pain for

Tarrellton's suffering. "God turned his back on Jesus so his pure eyes wouldn't have to see it," I sneered, again not sure the words were mine. I recognized an old anger tied to my own father's rejection of me. "And he turned his back on Lucretia and her children," I finished.

"Sweetheart, turn it all over to the Lord," Tom said quietly. "This weird situation. The old bitterness. The lonely, lost, little girl feelings I see in your eyes sometimes. Open your heart to the One who can heal it all!"

Shaken by the intensity of his pleading, I turned my back on him and on the God who, I felt, had been totally unresponsive to such suffering as Lucretia had borne and, yes, as I had borne throughout the lonely, empty years of my growing up. I stood staring blindly out the kitchen window until I heard Tom leave the room.

Suddenly, though I had been the one to reject him, I could not bear the bleak emptiness of the room without him. I rushed into the hallway and stopped uncertainly. Then I heard his low voice coming from the living room. Standing in the doorway, I could see him sitting in his big leather chair, his head resting in his hands, obviously praying, although I couldn't make out the words.

I retraced my steps to the kitchen. Tom didn't need me. The need was all on my side, always had been. I felt a thrust of resentment that this was so, that Tom's love and need for me would always come second to his love and need for his God.

Though I had never felt any particular closeness to him, I had always believed God exists. Until I met Tom, I had felt that was enough. But, from the first,

I had sensed that Tom had something I didn't, some inner peace and joy that I had never known. And though he had often tried to share it with me, I had felt no need for anything more than Tom's love. Now Lucretia's unmet needs, joined with my old bitterness, were breeding within me a contempt for the God Tom adored.

"Come with me to prayer meeting at the little church up the road, Manda." Tom said from the kitchen doorway. His eyes held longing, but beneath it I noticed that peace had replaced his fears. His God was sufficient, as always. It gave me a lonely, shut-out feeling, but the longing in his eyes told me how much he wanted me to go with him.

"All right," I agreed and was amazed at the happiness that lit his face. Second-best or not, I had to admit that he loved me.

My head throbbed as I dressed in an emerald green wool outfit that, I knew, turned my eyes the same shade. I ignored the headache, smoothing a little extra blush onto my cheeks to compensate for the dark circles the pain was drawing beneath my eyes.

I didn't look forward to going to church, but maybe the human contact would be good for me, maybe lift me out of my depression. I had little hope that the service would do any more for me than Reverend Lawson's dry social sermons ever had.

Little did I expect to experience the next episode in the life of Lucretia Adams while at church!

TWELVE

It was almost seven-thirty when Tom parked the car with the dozen or so others in the parking lot in front of the church. I kept my eyes averted from the cemetery, concentrating on the few people going down the walk ahead of us and into the narrow white frame building.

Inside, a gold-carpeted aisle separated two sets of plain wooden pews, some of them marked with brass nameplates. Tom and I took a seat on an unmarked pew near the back of the half-filled church.

The atmosphere was warm and friendly, partly because of the people who kept stopping by to shake our hands and welcome us and partly due to the golden wood that paneled the walls and formed the raised platform on which stood the lectern. On each side of the platform, a wooden pedestal held what looked like an oil lamp.

"Tom," I whispered, "are those *oil* lamps?"

"Looks like it," he answered doubtfully.

The woman in front of us turned around. "I couldn't help overhearing," she said with a friendly smile. "They *are* oil lamps and have been on those same stands for over a hundred fifty years. Of course, they're used now only in case of power failure, but once they were the only source of light in the building. My grandmother used to clean the chimneys, trim the wicks, and see that they were filled with oil every week before meeting. I heard her tell about it many times."

"The church has been here since Civil War times, then?" I put in eagerly, avoiding Tom's eyes.

"Oh, yes, and a good many years before that," she said proudly. "Of course, it's been remodeled some over the years, but underneath the paneling and the carpet, it's the same old log building that was built at the time of the Great Revival in 1801."

"How interesting!" I exclaimed, hoping she would continue, but she turned around to face the front, and I saw that a stocky, red-haired Tom Sawyer type had mounted the platform.

"Page 471," he announced in a voice that carried easily to the back of the room. Conversations died abruptly, and there was a scurrying for songbooks and a rustling of pages.

Tom smiled at me and held out the opened book for me to share. " 'Wonderful love that rescued me, sunk deep in sin . . . ,' " he sang loudly with the others in his reasonably true baritone. The song was unfamiliar to me, and I let my thoughts wander.

Over a hundred years ago, did a pew have the name "Adams" engraved on its brass plate? I wondered. Had Lucretia and her family sat here Sunday after Sunday raising their voices in song?

" '. . . Raising my soul from out the dead, love found a way!' " Tom sang beside me. The words, eerily out of context to my wandering thoughts, sent a chill down my spine. I listened intently to the next lines:

> *Love found a way to redeem my soul,*
> *Love found a way that could make me whole;*
> *Love sent my Lord to the cross of shame,*
> *Love found a way . . .*

If only love, or something, could find a way to go back through the years and help Lucretia, I thought, *but it's too late for that now.* I could do absolutely nothing for her. Whatever tragedies she had endured were long since over, and her weary body had been at rest for over a hundred years.

Not her soul, though, I thought. Neither love nor anything else had put that tormented soul at peace, or she would not still be haunting this valley on Deserter's Creek.

"Notice that second verse," Tom Sawyer interrupted. " 'Love bridged the gulf twixt me and heaven. . . .' Folks, that's just exactly what God did when Satan influenced Adam and Eve to rebel against him and dig the first part of the chasm that has separated God and man ever since. He loved mankind so much he sacrificed his only Son to build a bridge that can carry you and me across that chasm back to fellowship with our Creator."

The red-haired man was saying the same thing Tom had said this afternoon—that we must make a con-

scious choice to have any kind of relationship with
God. But where did that leave those of us who had
not made such a choice? Tom had said Lucretia might
have thought she could "blunder through life without
making a choice at all." Did that leave her in neutral
territory, or did it mean that, by not choosing God,
she had automatically chosen Satan?

"Redemption is a universal need," the song leader
was saying, "that can be met only by deliberately
renouncing the rebellious spirit that lies inherent in
Adam's race and acknowledging Jesus Christ as Lord
and Savior. Acts 4:12 tells us, '. . . There is none other
name under heaven given among men, whereby we
must be saved.' And when we call upon that name,
as the song says, we are redeemed, set free, forgiven.
'Love found a way!' Let's sing it!"

Wait a minute! I thought. *Maybe it's not quite that
simple for some of us.* The red-haired man had an
open, freckle-faced innocence that had probably never
known a rebellious or bitter thought in all his thirty-
odd years. But had he ever experienced the loneliness
of a rejected child? Had he ever known the grief and
despair of a Lucretia Adams?

What is it her restless soul seeks? I wondered. *For
what purpose has she shown me those anguished
scenes from the past? Is there something she wants
me to do for her?*

" 'Love found a way to redeem my soul,' "Tom sang.
They were back to the chorus.

Lucretia, I would help you if I could find the way,
I told her silently. *If only I knew what it is you want!*

It was growing dim inside the church, I noticed,
in spite of the electric globes overhead. Perhaps they

would have a chance to use those patient oil lamps after all. The power was certainly weaker than it had been when we came in.

The windows were high and impossible to see out of, and I supposed that was to keep wandering eyes and minds on the preacher. But what I could see of the sky seemed as bright as midmorning, much lighter than it should have been at this hour at this time of year. I wondered why the light did not penetrate more into the dimness inside, or why they didn't light the oil lamps before the artificial light failed altogether. . . .

. . . *Then I saw it sitting there on its draped sawhorses between the lampstands. The sickly odor of dying lilies assaulted my senses. The now slowed, mournful rhythm of the singing began a painful throbbing in my head.*

The singing stopped, and the minister took his place in the pulpit behind the coffin. He placed an open Bible on the lectern and solemnly looked out over the congregation from beneath bony gray brows. He lifted one thin, pale hand and began to read, " 'Remember now thy Creator in the days of thy youth. . . .' "

His voice faded in and out of my consciousness. My eyes sought Joel's cold, still face. Surely this was a nightmare from which I would awaken to find him warm and alive beside me. But never again would Joel. . . . Oh, Joel, how can I bear it? I thought. Panic rose in me.

I forced my thoughts back to the reading of the Scripture: " 'Then shall the dust return to the earth as it was. . . .' "

No! That's worse! *Frantically, I searched for some thought, some safeguard against hysteria.*

Where the sawhorses now stood, we had stood, Joel and I—he in his best suit and I in my striped silk dress with the white woolen shawl. Ma had knitted the shawl for me because the silk was thin and it would be cold in the church, she had said. And it had been cold, but I had been too wrapped in Joel's love—that showed so plainly in his eyes when he looked at me—to pay any mind to the weather.

Oh, Joel! *A sob escaped me.* I'll bring you flowers, something fresh and clean-smelling, not sickly sweet with the scent of dying like these lilies. I'll never be able to bear lilies again.

"*My friends, we are gathered here on this sad occasion to. . . .*"

The reading was over. Now there were only the eulogy and prayers to sit through before we would be outside in the churchyard. And that would mean leaving Joel there alone.

I'll come every day, *I vowed.* But Joel will no more be here than he is in that cedar box.

Where is Joel? *I wondered.* Can he see us now? Is he somewhere watching as we pay our "last respects"?

Respects? How many here had come out of respect for Joel? I looked around at the people who filled the little church. Certainly not Sophie Miller whose son rode with Morgan and whose husband had been killed at Perryville! Even as her plump hands patted me soothingly, her scornful eyes had said clearly, "My man's dead, too, but at least he died honorably."

And there sat pious William and Martha Smith acting like butter wouldn't melt in their mouths. I had heard William say sternly, "He's committed the unpardonable sin."

William Smith and Sophie Miller were Confederate sympathizers. They had hated Joel ever since he joined the Union Army. They were glad for an excuse to condemn him, and the others followed along like so many sheep. I hated them all!

Even the minister with his soft words and golden promises showed his doubt of Joel's salvation. Joel had accepted what the minister called God's plan of salvation in this very church when he was twenty years old and had been baptized in the creek that same Sunday. Yet, because he hated killing, he was condemned.

That was one reason I had chosen the verse from John 5:24 to be engraved on his stone: ". . . He that heareth my word, and believeth on him that sent me, hath everlasting life, and shall not come into condemnation; but is passed from death unto life."

Joel's mother had wanted his grave marked with a cross, but to me a cross represented death. Joel had loved life, and even though his father was paying for the stone, I had insisted on the one with the squirrel. Joel had never liked hunting and had done so only when our need for meat had made it necessary. Never had he killed for pleasure, and I knew, as surely as I knew my own nature, that Joel had not taken his own life.

Someone was taking my arm, leading me to the trestles with their terrible, beloved burden. I leaned over and kissed his cold cheek, then held Susannah as she kissed him good-bye. She was screaming, but I hardly realized it as someone took her from me.

The boys were led away, Harrison's silent sobs jerking his sturdy body and Tarrellton's face red and swollen with repressed grief.

I can't let them close that lid! They can't seal him away from me! *But they were taking me away, urging me gently, but firmly down the aisle. Then we were outside, and the bright sunlit morning was an insult to my grief.*

Behind me, I could hear the pallbearers' footsteps made heavy on the wooden floor by the burden they carried. We stood aside as they passed, then fell into line behind the box, closed and impersonal-looking in the hands of the six men. I tried to pretend that what they carried was an empty box, but they staggered under its weight, and my heart, also riding in that box, added to their load.

I was numb, resigned to what must come—the throwing in of the first clods of dirt, my leaving without him. I didn't notice that the bearers had passed the cemetery until I stumbled on clumps of the higher grasses that grew outside the fence. The open grave yawned up at me from outside the fence beside the road.

My grief-numbed brain was slow to understand until I heard someone explain this unheard-of thing to someone else: "He killed hisself. He can't be buried in holy ground."

"No!" I screamed. "No! No! You can't do this to him! He is innocent!"

They were trying to quiet me, to comfort me—all the good hypocrites who had met in secret and decided this terrible thing. I could see by the set look of Ma and Pa Adams' lips and the bleakness in their eyes that they had known, even though they weren't happy with the decision.

"What does it matter, Lu?" Pa Adams was saying in my ear. "The boy's dead. He won't know or care where they put him. Leave it be!" But this last insult to Joel's decency was more than I could stand.

I pushed them all away from me and ran to stand between him and the yawning grave. My voice was amazingly calm as I spoke. "So long as there's breath in my body, you will not put him in this grave!"

I heard shocked gasps and furtive whisperings. "She's gone mad!" they said.

Let them whisper. I was saner now than I'd been since I'd heard that fatal crack from the captain's rifle in the woods behind our house. I would stand here until I died and joined him before I would let them put that box where all who passed would see and remember the captain's lies which everyone was so ready to believe.

If only I were a man! I thought with longing. Then I would hunt that captain and shoot him down like the dog he is, the way he shot Joel, without trial or mercy.

All at once, I knew what to do. "I want some men to dig a grave on my own land," I said, still calm and reasonable in this condition I had reached somewhere beyond grief. No doubt the grief would return, but now I must get done what I had decided to do. We would have our own private graveyard—Joel, the children, and I—in the woods where only rough stones marked the burial places of my father's slaves from years past. I would notify the monument maker to bring the stone to the woods instead of to the churchyard.

The place was mine, inherited from my father, and no one could tell me what to do there. And in a sense, it was hallowed ground, for the slaves had held their own religious ceremonies over their dead. It had been several years since my father had buried his last slave and set the rest free, but I still remembered their mournful singing around that last grave.

Joel's parents had never owned slaves. Joel had joined the Union Army because he believed slavery was wrong. Yes, he could rest there with the wronged black people better than he could near those who had wronged him. I would demand that when I died they bury me beside him.

"If no one will help me, I will dig it myself," I told their staring faces. I saw that they believed me. Even though I didn't look back, I knew they were all following, some of them out of curiosity perhaps, but there would be enough men to dig that grave in the woods. . . .

They were singing again, and the music throbbed in my head: " 'Amazing grace, how sweet the sound, that saved a wretch like me. . . .' "

We were inside the church again, and the room was bright. The high windows were mirrors quick-silvered with the darkness outside.

"Love found a way" seemed more appropriate to me. Love had found a way to save Joel from that final humiliation, and love would find a way to be with him. . . .

" '. . . Was blind but now I see,' " the deep voice

beside me sang lustily. I realized it was Tom's. He reached over and took my hand without looking at me. I was Amanda, and my headache was receding.

"Now I see," my thoughts echoed the words of the song. Lucretia had shown me why Joel was buried in the woods. Perhaps this was what she had wanted all along—to have someone know and sympathize and maybe honor her dishonored husband's grave.

The funeral I had just witnessed was the first time one of her scenes had been out of chronological order, but then this was the first time I had been inside the church. This time, I hadn't acted out the scene, or, at least, I didn't think I had. I glanced at Tom, whose eyes crinkled pleasantly with those sun lines I loved. He seemed happy as he shook hands with various people. Apparently, I had done nothing to embarrass him.

Did this mean Lucretia's power was less, now that she was satisfied? Could she rest now?

As Tom and I left the church amid handshakes and introductions and invitations to come again, I felt lightheaded with relief. Now that I knew the whole story, I felt sure Lucretia's purpose in "haunting" me had been met and we could part company, mutually satisfied.

I'll see that his grave is honored, Lucretia, I promised silently as we passed the graveyard on our way to the car. *I'll keep it clean and plant flowers, and you will be able to rest.*

If I had listened then, would I have heard Lucretia's mocking laughter?

THIRTEEN

The next morning, Chad was knocking on the door before I had washed the breakfast dishes.

"I'm ready to work out the money you gave Mama the other day," he said belligerently.

"But you don't—"

"It was too much," he interrupted. "Even Brother Jimmy says so." From the determined look on his face, I decided not to argue.

"All right. Come on back to the kitchen and I'll tell you what I want done." I went back to the sink, squirted dish detergent into the water, and put the glasses and silverware into the hot suds. "Now," I said, drying my hands on the towel and turning to Chad just in time to see him quickly avert hungry eyes from the leftover bacon and scrambled eggs I had been about to scrape out for Black Night.

"Let's have some breakfast," I substituted for what I had started to say, wondering how I would swallow another breakfast so soon after I had eaten. This had been one of those rare days when I had eaten with Tom. But I knew better than to offer to fix breakfast for Chad alone. "Then we'll get at that compost I've been wanting to start."

Chad looked at the two revealing dirty plates on the table, then glanced at me reproachfully. I felt my face flush.

"I done eat," he mumbled, looking away.

"All right," I surrendered again, my voice falsely bright, like a nurse trying to humor a difficult patient. "But I'll expect you for lunch." Before he could refuse, I added, "I always fix lunch for workhands. Now, Chad," I hurried on, "I want you to rake up leaves from the woods and carry them in baskets to that place by the garden where I've been piling wood ashes from the fireplace."

He nodded, asked where to get the rake and the baskets, and went out whistling.

All through the morning, I found myself drawn to the windows to watch him at his work. It was a real pleasure having him out there, and I enjoyed baking a chocolate cake with chocolate icing and fixing other food I thought he might enjoy for lunch.

Tom and I would have to talk about children soon, either some of our own or some to adopt. I would have liked having Chad. His home life was so poor I knew I could do better by him—feed and clothe him, see that he stayed in school where, come to think of it, he should have been today.

Chad had a mother, though, such as she was. From my own childhood feelings for my indifferent father, I knew better than to try to separate him from her.

But I could feel my fondness for prickly, independent Chad growing as rapidly as the pile of leaves he was making by the garden.

Tom called just before noon to say he had taken the afternoon off but was staying in town to try to locate an office he could rent. When we hung up, I called Chad to lunch.

At my suggestion, he went to the bathroom to wash up. He came back, sat down at the kitchen table, bowed his head, closed his eyes, and moved his lips in what I assumed was a silent grace. Then he ladled mashed potatoes, baked beans, and fried apples onto his plate. I handed him a couple of ham sandwiches.

"You got any ketchup?" he asked with his mouth full. I handed him the bottle and watched in dismay as he drowned everything in it except the apples. I suppressed an involuntary shudder as he took a mouthful of ketchup-covered mashed potatoes. "Ummm!" he said appreciatively, and I grinned back at him.

When he had started on his third plateful and his eating had slowed a bit, he looked up. "The com . . . whatever you call it . . . is comin' along fine." He showed no resentment or belligerence now. He was a workman satisfied that he was giving a dollar's labor for a dollar's pay.

"Good!" I answered. "I'll come out and help you shred and mix it after a while." Tom had said we could shred it with the lawn mower. "But don't you think you've done enough to call it even on the ten? I'll be glad to pay. . . ."

The sullen look closed down again. I could have kicked myself! Would I never learn?

"OK, Chad," I apologized, setting a piece of chocolate cake in front of him. "But let's get one thing straight between us. I won't give you anything, but I don't want you working for me for nothing, either. That makes *me* feel guilty. Understand?"

He stared at the cake thoughtfully for several seconds, then nodded. "OK. Only I can't help you on Saturdays. I start this week cleaning the church every Saturday."

I wanted to ask him why he wasn't in school today, but I felt that he had stayed out to pay what he thought of as a debt to me. Instead, I said teasingly, "You'll be a rich man soon, Chad, with all this work."

He nodded solemnly. "But it ain't just the money. Ever since I got saved a few weeks ago, I been looking for somethin' I could do for Jesus. Brother Jimmy says cleanin' the church is a good place to start. He says he used to do it when he was about my age."

I tried to picture the minister from Wednesday evening's service, but all I could recall was the old man who had preached Lucretia's husband's funeral. The only person I remembered from the real service was Tom Sawyer, the song leader. Caught up in Lucretia's story, I had missed the rest of the service.

"Your Brother Jimmy sounds like a nice man," I said, "and he seems to have a lot of faith in you, Chad."

He nodded. "He's cool!" he said admiringly. "Mama says he's too young and innocent looking to know much, but Brother Jimmy used to drive an eighteen-wheeler before he got the call to preach. I reckon he knows just about everything there is to know!"

He polished off the last of his cake and got up from the table without thanking me or excusing himself.

"See you got a dog," he said as he started to the door.

"Yes. His name is Black Night."

"I wouldn't get too attached to him if I was you," Chad warned.

"Why not?"

"Oh, he'll most likely get run over or something," he said matter-of-factly. Then he was out the door before I could question his pessimistic attitude. I watched from the window as Chad played with Black Night, even though he didn't think the dog would be around long.

What a strange child he was! Or had he ever really been a child? Being more or less on his own had made him mature early. Sometimes, it seems childhood is skipped almost entirely. The natural, spontaneous gaity of children is hard to come by. A person becomes strangely old and suspicious of other people's motives, as Chad was and as I had been.

Watching his rare abandonment in his play with the dog, I vowed to do everything in my power to see that he experienced some childhood while it was still the proper time for it. And watching him hug himself against the chill, I vowed that, if I could keep him working for me, he would have a proper meal any time I could coax him to eat, and some warm clothes, too. I wondered if his mother would buy him anything with the ten dollars, or if she would spend it on herself. Surely she would let him keep whatever he made cleaning the church.

Again, I wished that Chad were mine, but I put the thought from me, not so much because it was wrong to covet the child, but because it seemed impossible to have him. The thought depressed me, though, and when I began cleaning the kitchen, I felt the now-familiar headache returning. As I worked, my depression grew. . . .

. . . I will protect his fierce pride somehow, *I vowed.* I'll never let him or any of them feel ashamed because of their father. They won't go to school ragged or barefoot, and they will carry good lunches in their lunch pails if I have to work until my hands bleed!

Only there was so little work in the winter months. In the growing season, I could hire out to the farmers to work in the crops, no matter what Joel's parents said about it. Or I could help the women with feeding the hands or with canning or other harvest work. But in the winter months, I could find so little to do. The washing and ironing the Lafontaines gave me to do was as near charity as the occasional hand- outs I was forced to take from Ma and Pa Adams. My own parents likely were spinning in their graves at the thought of their daughter working as a hired hand or on charity, but there was nothing else to do.

Oh, I'd be glad when summer came again! In the hot summer days, even the Lafontaine children went barefoot, and there was food from the garden. I would can and preserve more than ever this year, if I could get planting seed and preserving sugar and other supplies. We could live on these things and do without the extras. I could help the Adamses and Lafontaines with hog killing and earn meat for those lunches I was determined my children would have, even if we had to do without meat most of the time at home. And I would work out and earn money for shoes and books.

Susannah was young; she didn't quite realize. And Harrison was a good, sensible boy. He would accept whatever I found necessary to do, or do without. He would take the hardships and become a man because of them. Nothing about him was frivolous or even imaginative. He was a good, steady boy who would make a good, steady man like his Grandpa Adams, although he looked more like me.

Tarrellton, though—my heart turned over at the thought of him. He didn't complain any more than Harrison did. He would grit his teeth and bear whatever we had to bear. At home, he was always the first to say he wasn't hungry when food was short. But his self-respect shriveled a little with every public humiliation, such as the outgrown coat I had forced him to wear to school. The pride that had held his head high through it all so far and had caused so many black eyes over the teasing about his papa at school would be chipped away little by little. And when it was gone, the fiercely independent, intensely alive being I loved so much would be destroyed.

The other two had enough of their grandfather's stoicism to accept and adjust. And their grandpa could not understand about Tarrellton who looked so much like Joel and yet was so little like him.

"Let him learn that life is hard," his grandpa had told me. "He has too much pride as it is." But to take away Tarrellton's pride was to destroy the boy himself, and I would rather see him dead like his father than see that bright flame imprisoned in some dreary half-life of drudgery and dullness.

Outside, he had gone back to his work, the dog

frisking at his heels. He looked like a little old man, a boy trying to do a man's work. *If only I could spare him more. . . .*

I'd rather see him entirely dead than half alive. *The thought seemed locked in my aching brain. I had prayed that never again would I have to suffer the pain of parting from one I loved. Was this my punishment for that obscene prayer—to watch him pale into a shadow of himself and drudge through the years half alive?*

For the first time, I realized that there are worse things than death. I still missed Joel achingly, but wasn't it selfish to wish him back when Joel himself surely was infinitely better off? No more agonizing decisions of kill or not kill, no more being branded a coward because of his convictions.

Wouldn't Tarrellton, too, be better off sent to heaven with his soul intact than to let it wither and shrink within him here? The thought came, so beautiful in its simplicity. (If only I could be sure there was a heaven.) Though it would be like tearing my heart out all over again to give him up, wasn't I being selfish not to set him free before he was destroyed bit by bit?

My head hurt so! If only it would stop so I could think!

There was a knocking at the back door, and I stiffened, feeling the beginning of panic as I glanced out the window and saw that he was gone. Where was he? Had something happened to him? I flew to the door and threw it open. He stood on the doorstep, holding a rake in cold-reddened hands.

"I'm ready for you to show. . . ." *He let the words*

*trail off as he stared at me. His eyes widened into
trapped dark pools of fear.*

*"Tarrellton—," I began, but he gave one strangled
yelp, turned, and ran.*

"Come back, Tarrellton!" I shouted.

*He looked back once from the corner of the house,
then ran on as though the devil were after him. I
tried to follow, but the pain beat at my brain, para-
lyzing me. I sank down on the grass, drifting with
the pain and the exhaustion that enveloped me. . . .*

. . . The first drops of rain awakened me. I was stiff
and chilled from lying on the cold, damp ground. My
head still hurt, though not quite so fiercely, and I
was bone tired. I managed to get up and go inside
the house. I dragged myself to the bathroom, swallowed a couple of Bufferin, then took a hot bath.

The rain was falling heavily now. Together with the
hot bath, it eased my tension, and the headache became more bearable.

As I finished dressing, Tom came in excitedly an-
nouncing that he had rented office space on the
square behind the courthouse. "It's already vacant,
and it's furnished," he rattled on, unaware of my
preoccupation. "And since I've already trained a re-
placement, I think I'll go ahead and take the plunge,
if you don't mind going hungry for a while."

I winced, thinking of Lucretia and her little family,
but I nodded my head at him and forced a smile.
"You'll make the best lawyer this town has ever seen!"
I predicted. "And you'll be right here in town if I. . . ."
I started to say "need you," but changed it to "get
lonesome."

Tom hugged me. "My granddad was the best lawyer

this town has ever seen," he corrected. "If I can be half the lawyer, or half the man, he was, I'll be more than satisfied. But it will be good to see 'Thomas Farris, Attorney at Law' on a shingle on the square again! I've already ordered my sign."

Tom was so excited about his new venture, I tried to forget the day's trip into the past and be jubilant with him. I did tell him about Chad, though, and the pride he had taken in his work and how eagerly he had eaten his mashed potatoes with ketchup on them. Only once did I slip and start to call him Tarrellton, but I caught myself in time. It brought back my feelings of the afternoon when I had watched Chad at his work, confusing him with that other boy of a hundred years ago.

I shrank from recalling the look of pure horror on Chad's face as he had stared at me from the back door. *What did he see in my face to frighten him so?* I wondered. We had been on such good terms only a short while before. Had Lucretia's disquieting thoughts of Tarrellton's death shown in my face? Or had Chad simply looked at me and seen Lucretia?

I pushed aside the horrifying thought that Lucretia might have taken me over so completely that I had even looked like her. It was unthinkable that I might harm Chad, just as it was unbelievable that Lucretia had entertained thoughts of "mercy killing" of her beloved Tarrellton. But how could I know what Lucretia had been capable of doing? And how could I know what *I* might do under her influence?

Nonsense! I told myself. She had never influenced me in any way, except to show me how the house should be built, which I hardly admitted seriously. She had merely shown me, in a very vivid way, the story of her life here on Deserter's Creek. Even if I granted her that much power, which I still thought might be scientifically explainable, I couldn't believe she had the power to do anything more. Surely Chad had had no reason to be afraid of me this afternoon!

After supper, Tom busied himself in a brief he was preparing, and I picked up the last of the books I had brought home from the library. The others had mostly been concerned with flickering lights in graveyards, floating white or black shapes that appeared to various people as warnings or in times of stress, and unidentified flying objects that landed in cornfields.

Several chapters in one book had been devoted to some nuns who did gymnastics and shouted obscenities and were considered demon possessed. Other chapters discussed men and women who turned into animals at the full moon, or other childish fantasies. There had been nothing that remotely resembled my experiences here at Deserter's Creek.

The last book was also about possession, and I was about to lay it aside when I came on a chapter entitled, "Possession for Vengeance." It told of a young married woman who was possessed by the spirit of a girl who had been murdered. The girl's body and her killer had never been discovered. Through the young wife, the girl's spirit sought revenge. When the body was discovered and the killer was brought to justice, the spirit had left the woman in peace.

Though closer to my experiences, this still did not fit my situation. The people who had wronged Joel

Adams had been dead before I was born. What purpose could Lucretia have in trying to possess me? If only I could know what she wanted!

"What are you reading, sweetheart?" Tom's question broke into my thoughts.

I didn't want to tell him, but he came over to stand behind my chair and read over my shoulder. I sat there dreading his outburst, but he merely reached over and tousled my hair.

"I thought you had conjured up enough ghosts around here without reading about more of them!"

"I think you're right," I agreed, laying the book on the lamp table and smiling up at him. I wanted the safe, warm feeling of his arms around me tonight, and I wasn't going to do anything to alienate him.

FOURTEEN

Friday dawned gloomy and rainy—a summer-definitely-has-ended kind of day. Depression was in the air, but I had no time for Lucretia today, and I hoped she would leave me alone.

I drove into town early and picked up the things I wanted for supper, deciding on a beef roast with carrots and potatoes, a tossed salad with my own curry dressing, green beans, rolls, a gelatin salad, and a German chocolate cake for dessert—all inelegant but homey food I thought Mr. Roberts might like. If he lived alone, he would enjoy a home-cooked meal.

I stopped in Tom's new office for a moment, profusely admiring the sagging leather couch and chair in the tiny waiting room. I promised to make new drapes for the windows of the even smaller inner office with its scarred wooden desk and beige metal file cabinets.

Tom opened one of the file drawers and proudly showed me two folders neatly labeled with the names of clients.

"One wants a will and the other a deed," he confessed, "but word is getting around. And I still have half a dozen cases I'm handling for the old firm. I'm going to have to hire a part-time secretary. Do you know where I might find one who would meet my requirements?"

"37-23-36, green eyes, and black hair?" I suggested.

"Perfect!" he agreed. He pulled me to him. "But she'd have to pass a proficiency test." He kissed me once, held me at arm's length as though seriously studying my qualifications, then kissed me again, longer and not so lightly this time.

"I think you'll do, ma'am," he said huskily. "When can you start?"

A knock on the outer door made me jump guiltily.

Tom laughed. "When you play a part, you enter into it completely, don't you, sweetheart? You're my wife, remember?" He deliberately kept his arm around me as he called, "Come in!"

"Oh, shoot!" Tom said. "I was going to tell whoever it was that I was just trying out a new secretary, but you've met Amanda, haven't you, Dare?"

"How about me tryin' her out next?" Daren asked, leering at me.

"Amanda," Tom said sternly, "I think you'd better go home!"

"All right," I agreed. "I'll see you and Lisa tonight, won't I, Daren?"

"You bet!" he answered.

"I'll give your proposition serious thought, sir," I

said to Tom as I picked up my purse and raincoat from the chair.

"And if you don't like his offer, my establishment is just across the square," Daren reminded me.

I smiled at Tom. "I like everything about him," I said confidentially to Daren as I was leaving. "But I'll keep your offer in mind, too, sir, just in case."

"On second thought, I may hire a blonde," Tom called after me.

"And I may scratch her eyes out!" I called back. I heard them both laughing as I went through the narrow hallway and down the stairs to the street.

Tom's lighthearted banter and the love I knew lay behind it gave me a warm feeling that not even the miserable weather outside could dampen. I found myself smiling broadly at a red-haired man who was entering the stairway as I left it.

"Why, hello, Mrs. Farris," he said with a crooked grin that seemed vaguely familiar, though I couldn't quite place him. "I was on my way to see your husband to extend an official welcome," he went on, "but I guess it should be the other way around, since he's been a part of this town much longer than I have."

"I remember you!" I exclaimed. "You're the song leader at the Deserter's Creek church!"

His grin slipped a little, but he soon had it back in place. "I can see that my sermon Wednesday evening must have been memorable!" he laughed. "I'm also the minister. It's a low-budget church!"

"Oh, I'm so sorry!" I stammered. "I didn't realize—"

"Mrs. Farris," he interrupted, "seriously now, how could you remember my mediocre singing and not know that I also preached that evening, even if you don't recall what I was sure was at least a semi-immortal sermon? Did you sleep through my message?"

I could feel my face growing red. "I. . . ."

He laughed. "Forget it!" Then he groaned, and we both laughed at his choice of words.

"The local café may not look like much," he said, "but it's clean, and Mrs. Baker makes first-rate coffee. Could I treat you to a cup?"

I hesitated, charmed by his infectious grin and vivacious friendliness. Then I shook my head.

"A Coke, then?"

"I'm sorry. Could I take a raincheck? I really am in a hurry. We're having company. . . ."

"Of course," he agreed quickly. "But remember, a red-headed Irishman named Jimmy O'Brien owes you one."

Chad's "Brother Jimmy." I had forgotten that, too. "I promise not to sleep through your next semi-immortal sermon," I called back impulsively as I started across the street. "And I hear you drive a mean eighteen-wheeler, too!"

"What . . . ?" he began. Then the puzzled frown crisscrossing the freckles cleared. He shook his head. "That Chad!" He was laughing as he went up to Tom's office.

A nice man, I thought as I got into Annabel and drove toward home. *No wonder Chad thinks so highly of him.* I was glad Chad had someone like Jimmy O'Brien in his life. I felt that he would be easy to talk to about almost anything. He certainly was unlike any minister I had ever known!

But how would he react to a recital of my experiences with Lucretia Adams? Would the crooked grin disappear, and the frank blue eyes uncharacteristically avoid mine? Would he retract that offer to buy me a cup of coffee? Somehow I didn't think so. I felt that Chad's "Brother Jimmy" would at least give me an unbiased hearing. That was something I had not found since I had first seen that gray house.

The thought gave me a good feeling. I found myself singing snatches of songs the rest of the way home and as I began my gelatin salad, put the roast on, got the cake in the oven, and straightened the house. By three-thirty, I had frosted the cake and was ready to set the table.

The rain had stopped, so I put on a brown suede jacket and scarf and went outside in search of something for a centerpiece. A faint mist rose eerily from the creek, its green pools stained brown at the edges with fallen sycamore leaves. It seemed gloomier than ever, and I walked quickly up the road beside the blacktop.

All the pretty leaves had fallen under the weight of the rain and were soggy and unusable. Still, though my brown wool slacks and sweater felt warm under the jacket, the cool, damp air did not encourage a leisurely walk. Finally, I broke off a spray of deep pink wahoo berries and some cedar and went back to the house. I felt thoroughly chilled and my spirits were as soggy and flat as the wet fallen leaves.

I turned at the front door and looked back down toward the road. The mist was still rising over the creek, swirling a little in the cold wind that had come up. I shivered, turned the doorknob, and went inside, wiping my wet loafers on the braid rug at the door.

I hurried into the kitchen, chose a small black metal tray and a bowl for the water, and began a Japanese arrangement with my cedar and wahoo. Just in case Lisa knew more about flowers than I did, I got out my book on flower arranging and followed directions closely, cutting three sprays of the cedar of varying heights and two of wahoo, one tall and one short.

Earth, man, and heaven, I thought as I placed the cedar in the traditional positions. "The Japanese flower for October is the chrysanthemum," I read, "which symbolizes immortality."

Well, I'll have to make do with wahoo, the berry used by the Indians, whatever it symbolizes.

The word immortality, however, stuck in my mind. It had a thrilling sound and meaning—to live forever, not as a mortal, but as something beyond this human state.

Tom would have explained it as existence with God in a perfect and beautiful life that never ended. But what about those who did not know God the way Tom felt he did? People like . . . Chad's mother, perhaps? Or Lucretia? Or me? Were all of us immortals-in-training? If so, where would the ungodly spend their immortality? Would they, like Lucretia, spend eons of time without a future, regretting the past in an endless limbolike now? Was Lucretia's existence as a wandering spirit, if that was what she was, just a time-filler until the Final Judgment, or was it the result of her judgment?

My head had begun the familiar ache that usually heralded a visit from her, but I fought it. Quickly, I put the wahoo in the arrangement, its shorter branch at the lower front to represent the Japanese "meadow" and its taller branch to the left and behind "heaven," slightly lower than my tallest cedar sprig to represent "mountain." I needed these earthy things to take my mind off the disturbing thoughts of life after death. Like a schoolchild unprepared for an exam, I didn't want to face immortality just yet.

My head throbbed dully, and my eyes began staring at the simple pink and green arrangement. Then it began to fade. . . .

. . . *The chipped brown teapot still had its tight, faded bouquet of yellow black-eyed Susans crushed into it. These were Susannah's favorite flowers. She thought they were named for her and brought them to me all during their blooming season as a special gift. Now they were dried and wilted, the stems brittle and the petals falling onto the tabletop like tears, as the white rosebush I had planted wept its petals over Joel's grave.*

The clock on the mantel in the parlor began its warning whirr. One, two, three, four—the tiny hammer struck the gong. . . .

. . . With a tremendous effort of will, I wrenched my thoughts away from Lucretia's. The teapot faded back into the low tray with its green and pink arrangement. The clock on the shelf over the kitchen table was my electric miniature grandmother clock. It said five o'clock! I simply didn't have time for Lucretia now!

As I checked the roast and vegetables in the Dutch oven, I felt jubilant that I had been able to stop her this time. Perhaps I always could have if I had wanted to badly enough. Or was it because she now knew I was interested, concerned, willing to listen?

As soon as I could, I planned to take flowers to the grave in the woods. *Maybe to hers, too,* I promised. Right now, though, I didn't have time for her.

FIFTEEN

I had just finished setting the table in the dining area when I heard Tom's car in the driveway. I carefully checked the living room and dining area. The pale pink cloth looked nice with my best gray and white china, and my cedar and wahoo centerpiece between pink candles in silver holders added just the right touch. This was our first attempt at entertaining in our new home, and I wanted to make a good impression on Tom's old friends. I wanted it to be a memorable occasion.

The evening turned out to be memorable, all right; Mr. Roberts saw to that! It was his evening from beginning to end. He was the first to arrive and the last to leave, and neither Daren's easy charm nor Lisa's bright friendliness was a match for Mr. Rob, as they all called him.

Lisa, one of those tall, thin females who can eat forty pounds of food and lose two pounds of fat, was an attractive girl with brown, naturally curly hair and an energetic enthusiasm that saw to it that she and I never lacked conversation. I was fascinated, though, by Mr. Rob's tales mostly about Lucretia Adams and our property here on Deserter's Creek, and found myself wishing Lisa would stop chattering and let me listen.

"I'd love to have the recipe for this curry dressing," Lisa said as she helped me clear the table and scrape dishes. "Did you see the way Dare piled it on his salad? And he a dyed-in-the-wool French dressing loyalist!"

"I'm glad you all liked it," I murmured, straining to hear what Mr. Rob was saying in the living room. "No, Lisa, don't bother with the dishes now. Let's spend the time together while you all are here. I'd much rather do them later."

She wasn't easy to persuade, but finally we joined the others over second cups of coffee.

"I recollect as plain as day the time that house burned," Mr. Rob was saying. "Me and a couple of fellers went fishin' down on the river the day before, and it was standin' there with its empty eye sockets— that's the windows. I always say a empty house has 'empty eye sockets.' "

Lisa winked at me, and I saw Daren roll his eyes.

"Anyway, the house was standin' there big as life one day," Mr. Rob went on, "and the next day was nothin' but a pile of ashes. There wasn't enough left of it to sweep up!"

"What caused the fire, Mr. Rob? You boys didn't have anything to do with it, did you?" Lisa asked Tom and Daren teasingly. "I remember one Halloween when you all were in high school, you and a couple of other guys burned down an old empty shack while Eleanor and I waited in the car, scared to death. . . ."

Both Daren and Tom were shaking their heads. "I don't even remember a house on this place," Tom said.

"Neither do I," Daren agreed. "I remember some guy starting to build here once. At least, he had some materials delivered. You remember, Lisa, we used to drive by here and park down by the river. . . ."

"Shut up, Daren!" she warned, laughing.

Daren laughed, too, and they exchanged a warm, intimate look that made me envious. I looked quickly at Tom, but Tom was eating the last of his favorite cake, and anyway, we had no such memories to share. Our own courtship had come along when we were both mature and "sensible," or at least more mature and sensible than a couple of teenagers. I had always been glad of that. Now, I wasn't so sure I hadn't missed something special.

"There's one thing I know," Lisa said. "I wouldn't have parked down by that creek! All those spidery tree limbs! You remember, Tom, how Eleanor and I both hated that spot?"

"How is Eleanor?" Tom asked.

"Fine," Lisa replied. "She's teaching, as she always planned to do. You know Paul was killed in Viet Nam early in the war?"

Tom nodded. "I was in Hong Kong and couldn't make it home, but I sent flowers and got a note back from Mrs. H."

My thoughts drifted. Had Tom and Eleanor Hobson parked on this dark, deserted road together? If it had been Eleanor sitting here opposite him tonight, would Tom's eyes have looked at her the way Daren's had at Lisa—warm and alight with pleasant memories of young love?

Mercifully, Mr. Rob's silken voice broke into my thoughts. "It's been gone since long before any of you was born." His voice dropped to a whisper. "There was some that said Lucretia Adams burned it herself." He paused dramatically.

"Oh? Well, did she?" Daren asked politely, his face settling back into the bored expression he had worn through most of Mr. Rob's tales.

"Nobody rightly knows, since she'd been dead for fifty years." Mr. Rob's eyes sparkled with excitement as he looked from one to another of us for our reaction.

Lisa laughed uncertainly. Daren rolled his eyes at Tom.

"Good grief, Mr. Rob," Tom burst out, "there's any number of reasons why an old house like that might burn! Lightning, spontaneous combustion, a tramp's fire. . . ."

Mr. Rob good-naturedly shrugged his thin shoulders. "Maybe. There wasn't no storm, no lightnin' out, but who knows about the rest? I'm just tellin' you what the talk was at the time. You see, this place has had a curse on it for a long time. There was the drownin' of Lucretia and her three children. . . ."

I gasped, and his keen, penetrating gaze was on me instantly.

"So that's what happened," I murmured. Then my heart froze in horror as I recalled Lucretia's feelings about Tarrellton. "Mr. Rob, it was . . . an accident, wasn't it? The drowning?"

"Oh, yes. No doubt about it. I heard my grandmother tell it a hundred times. It was the biggest tragedy ever to hit these parts in those days before the automobile came along to wipe out whole families in one blow."

"What happened?" Lisa asked. "Was the whole family drowned?"

"Yes. It must have been terrible." His voice was mournful. "And the worst part was, if they'd stayed in the house or gone out the back door and up the hill behind the house, they'd have been safe. After the flood, an old hen and chickens were found safe and dry under an old tub in the backyard just a little higher up the hill than the house itself. Lucretia and the children went out the front door. They musta been swept off their feet by the current, for the water wasn't really that deep here at the house. It never got into the house at all, just to the front door."

"How awful!" I whispered.

"Course of the creek has changed some since then," he said reassuringly. "It don't get up in the yard anymore. But the bodies were found down by the bridge, or where the bridge is now. Road used to run right through the creek. Lucretia still had one of them by the hand, they say. The other two was just a little ways down the creek."

I could feel tears burning my throat and eyelids. I could see it all so plainly—Susannah, Harrison, and Tarrellton—the laughing children playing in the creek, then their bodies swollen by its waters and bruised by the stones they had used to build their childish dams and playhouses.

"What were the children, boys or girls?" Lisa asked, her thoughts obviously on her four boys left with a sitter. I could tell by the look of horror on her face that she was identifying with Lucretia in her loss, or what would have been a loss if Lucretia had not drowned also. Lisa would have been even more horrified if she had known how dangerous sympathy for Lucretia could be.

"The oldest was a boy," Mr. Rob answered. "And I'm not sure, but I think the two least ones was girls."

"Two boys and a girl," I corrected absently. "Harrison was eleven, Tarrellton was ten, and Susannah was only seven. Tarrellton was her favorite. Mr. Rob, do you remember which one she . . . ?" Four pairs of eyes were staring at me. There wasn't a bored expression in the lot!

I laughed nervously, and Tom came to my rescue, but his eyes were troubled.

"There's this tombstone over in the churchyard that gives their names and ages," he explained. "Amanda's been imagining all sorts of things about that family ever since she visited that graveyard."

"Maybe old Lucretia's still around, Tom," Daren said, winking at me. "Maybe she tells Amanda these things."

"She—," I began.

"Don't be ridiculous!" Tom snapped. "Lucretia Adams has been dead for over a hundred years!"

Daren and Lisa exchanged startled glances. Mr. Rob's antenna quivered.

"That's what the stone says," he agreed, "but 'Where are Shakespeare's imagination, Bacon's learning, Galileo's dream?' " he quoted airily. " '. . . Methinks such things should not die and dissipate, when a hair can live for centuries, and a brick of Egypt will last three thousand years. I am content to believe that the mind of man survives, somehow or other, his clay.' Barry Cornwall," he explained to the rest of us who sat with our mouths open.

Lisa, Daren, and Tom were used to Mr. Rob's quotations, so perfectly and beautifully presented in that silken voice, and yet so incongruous with his normal colloquial speech. But even they were caught off guard by that one.

"What I'm gettin' at," he went on, "is there's some that believe Lucretia Adams ain't all that dead. Callie Palmer, for one. Her husband was gonna build a house on this property a few years back. That was after you left, Tom. Tarl inherited the property from his grandfather on his mother's side. He was a carpenter and he was gonna cut trees, have 'em sawed, and build it hisself. Only everything he did turned to tragedy. The last thing took his life. Callie sold the property as quick as she could.

"Jim Tupts was new around here then and of a skeptical nature, so he bought it. He said he'd build on it and live here, too. But Miz Tupts never did take to the place, though some said it was havin' Jim so close to Callie that bothered her. Callie was a looker in them days. Anyway, Miz Tupts made Jim build her a place in a subdivision, and he just held the property until you folks came along."

"But what happened to Callie Palmer's husband?" I asked, recalling Chad's comment: "That old lady killed my dad."

"A tree fell on him," Mr. Rob said somberly.

Daren and Tom snorted with laughter, and Lisa couldn't keep a straight face. I didn't see anything funny about it.

"That's how most of these so-called ghost stories get started," Tom said with that satisfied look he gets when he has been able to apply logic to some problem and solve it. "Mr. Rob, come on now! You know a tree could fall on anybody who tried to cut it, without any ghostly help."

Mr. Rob was shaking his head stubbornly, his thick, bony brows knit together in a frown. "Tarl Palmer had been a lumberman since he could walk, practically. His dad ran a sawmill. Tarl could make a tree fall on a chalk line. No, siree, Tom. You'll never convince Callie that tree just fell that way, backwards to all lumbering rules, against the cut. Of course, Tarl wouldn't a been in the way nohow if it hadn't been for the boy."

"Chad?" I asked.

He nodded. "Just a little feller he was then, four or five years old. Seems he followed his daddy that morning without Tarl knowin' it. Callie never was much of a mother. My guess is she was still in bed and didn't know where the kid was."

"But what happened?" Lisa asked.

"The kid darted right under that fallin' tree. Tarl, seein' the tree was fallin' backwards, jumped for the boy, threw him out of the way, but lost his balance and fell directly in the tree's path. A friend of his was comin' to help him that day and saw it all. He went for help, but it was too late. That tree was the granddaddy of all poplars. Every bone in Tarl's body was crushed."

I saw Lisa shudder, but my mind was busy with thoughts of Chad. Poor little kid! He had told me Lucretia had killed his father, but I hadn't realized he'd been there and had seen it happen. No wonder he was obsessed with death!

"Well, then, it was the little boy who actually caused the accident," Tom said, "and not your ghost, Mr. Rob."

"Some blamed the kid," Mr. Rob agreed, "though any fool would know he hadn't done it on purpose. Some blamed Callie for not watchin' him closer. One thing's sure, she ain't never been the same since. Went from bad to worse. The kid's been strange, too. He kept babblin' something about some 'old lady' showin' him a bird's nest that had fallen under the tree. The kid kept screamin', 'She wanted me to get 'em out, and now they're all broke!' He wouldn't talk about his daddy. Just them bird's eggs. Callie believed him. She swears to this day the whole thing was planned by Lucretia Adams."

"And any fool ought to know a woman who's been dead for over a hundred years had nothing to do with anything!" Daren said with a laugh.

Again, Mr. Rob was shaking his head. "Isaiah 57:20 says, 'The wicked are like the troubled sea, when it cannot rest, whose waters cast up mire and dirt.' I don't know how wicked Lucretia Adams was, but there's something about this place that's uneasy and has been ever since them people drowned. Call it whatever you want, but to my way of thinkin', it ain't no accident that everybody who tries to live here is discouraged, to put it mildly."

"And, yet, she let me build here," I put in absently,

my mind still on Chad and the horror of that day that haunted him even now. *"I didn't mean to! It was her! You gotta believe that!"* he had said to his father's grave. I knew now what he had meant. My heart yearned to help that little boy with his half-understood guilt feelings.

"Oh, good grief!" Tom exploded. He got up from the table, and Daren and Lisa rose also, hinting it was time to leave.

"Are you sure you don't want help with the dishes?" she asked again. "Then we'd better be getting back. This new sitter is young and has to be home early. Besides, I like to tuck the boys in. You and Tom come over now, hear? The supper was delicious," she added as they went out the door.

"I'll send you that curry dressing recipe," I promised.

"Oh, yes, do!" she responded quickly. " 'Bye!"

"Good night!" I called after them, resigned to the fact that I probably wouldn't be seeing much of Lisa. Even Daren's flirty eyes had avoided mine as they had said good-bye. Tom's reaction to Mr. Rob's ghost stories had them convinced that I was seeing and hearing things, as I had to admit I had been. As Tom walked them to their car, I couldn't help wondering if they would talk about us on the way home, feeling sorry for Tom and regretting that he and Eleanor, for whatever reason, had not made a go of it.

Mr. Rob broke into my thoughts with his thanks for the "de-licious supper," then said he had better be going too. "As Mr. Shakespeare says, '. . . Guests are often welcomest when they are gone.' "

"Not you, Mr. Rob," I said affectionately.

As I handed him his hat and coat from the hall closet, he leaned close and almost whispered, "Don't let them fool you, little lady. Matthew 27:52 and 53 says, 'The graves were opened; and many bodies of the saints which slept arose, and came out of the graves after his resurrection, and went into the holy city, and appeared unto many.' The Bible's full of 'ghost' stories. They couldn't be explained away then, and they can't now. And if you ever need a friend, you know where to find me." He winked at me as Tom came back inside. The two said good-bye, and Tom walked him to the door, patting him on his thin shoulder and asking him to come back sometime. When Mr. Rob's ancient Studebaker started up outside, however, Tom breathed an elaborate sigh of relief.

I busied myself with clearing the table of cake plates and coffee cups. I didn't share Tom's relief. It made me feel better just knowing I had a friend who would be neither amused nor skeptical about my experiences here.

As we prepared for bed, there arose outside a high, keening sound that, after my first startled reaction, I recognized as Black Night howling. But if Lucretia— or any other spirit—were out there, I was too tired to entertain her tonight!

SIXTEEN

Saturday morning, I awoke to another faintly throbbing headache and a deep depression. Since it was another dreary, overcast day, I assumed the headache was due to aching sinuses. I didn't know why I was so depressed. I had always loved a rainy day. Of course, it wasn't raining yet, but the sky promised rain soon. I supposed the fall rains had set in and I should accept the fact that the golden part of autumn was over. We were descending into winter, a season I hadn't liked much since I gave up making snowmen. *Perhaps this is the reason for my depression,* I thought.

Tom was already up, and I could hear water running in the bathroom. I jumped up, slipped into a robe, ran a comb through my hair, and went into the kitchen to start breakfast.

The automatic coffeepot I had filled the night before was hot, the red light shining cheerfully at me from the counter. Though not much of a coffee drinker, I poured myself a cup and sipped it black as I broke eggs into the skillet and buttered bread for the toaster.

I wouldn't be hungry for a couple of hours yet, and when I did eat, it would be something totally unbreakfasty—like chicken noodle soup or some of the leftover roast and salads from last night's supper. But Tom had to have eggs and toast, orange juice, coffee, cereal, bacon or sausage, or some other prosaic, predictable breakfast food every morning or he wasn't properly oriented for the day.

Tom, old buddy, I thought then, *you probably would have been a lot happier with somebody neat and orderly and predictable, somebody who goes to bed early and bounces up at the crack of dawn raring to go. A joiner of the Homemakers' and the Women's Club who could make important contacts for you. What you don't need,* I thought gloomily, *is a weirdo like me, a loner who stays up half the night reading or thinking or completing projects you didn't want started in the first place.*

Tom definitely didn't need someone who scared off all his friends by letting herself become involved with a woman who had been dead for a hundred years.

Tom's good-morning kiss on the back of my neck made me jump and spill coffee on the floor. "Penny for your thoughts," he teased.

I smiled at him over my shoulder as I grabbed for a paper towel. I might be unfocused and uncoordinated this early in the morning, but I was alert enough to know I loved Tom and I wasn't about to tell him what I had been thinking! I probably wasn't the type of wife he should have chosen, but I wasn't going to be the one to put doubts into his mind about it, at least not deliberately.

Suddenly, I wondered what kind of wife Eleanor Hobson would have made for Tom. The name conjured up an image of elegantly competent graciousness that made me wonder why Tom hadn't married her. Had it been just puppy love, or had there been something deeper between them? I wanted desperately to ask Tom about her, and yet I didn't want to mention her to him. I knew that once I said the name, she would be there between us, beckoning memories that might best be left sleeping. But how did I know he didn't think of her anyway, recalling with regret his lost love?

Stop being such an idiot, I scolded myself silently as I set Tom's plate before him and dropped a kiss on his bright hair before filling his coffee cup. You know he loves you. . . . *But does he love me the way he loved her?* my thoughts persisted.

I sat down at the table beside him while he offered thanks. Then I began to chatter about my plans for the day, smothering, with an inane flow of words, my jealous probing into Tom's past. This wasn't some long-dead stranger whose life was an interesting story. This was my husband, and maybe I would feel better if I didn't know too much about his past.

"I'm going in to the office for a while this morning," Tom said. "There's some work I want to get out. But I'll be home for lunch."

"Good!" I answered. "I'll fix something special."

He laughed and caught me to him, and I traced the laugh lines at the corners of his eyes with one finger.

"You're special enough for me," he said and gave me a long, lingering kiss that I knew would stay with me long after he had gone. I went to the door and stood watching as he drove away. I congratulated myself for not mentioning the name which Daren Blake had so innocently dropped into our conversation, the name that had caused such ripples of doubt in my assurance of Tom's love.

I washed Tom's breakfast dishes and those I'd left in the sink from supper and let them drain. The rain hadn't started yet, but twice I went to the front door to see if the roaring I heard was the creek. I couldn't see the water, so it was probably still flowing quietly over and around the rocks below the bridge. Perhaps the roaring was in my aching head.

The phone rang and I answered.

"Sweetheart," Tom's voice said, "I won't be home for lunch after all. Guess who I ran into in the drugstore a while ago? Eleanor Hobson and her mother! You remember, Lisa was talking about her last night? We used to have quite a thing going when we were kids." He laughed, and I could taste the bitter gall of jealousy. "I was in and out of their house constantly," he continued. "Mrs. Hobson was like a second mother to me. Her son, Paul, was a buddy of mine. He was killed in Viet Nam. I haven't seen them in years. I asked them both to lunch at the hotel. I didn't think you'd mind."

"Of course not, Tom," I managed to say.

"Would you like to come in and join us?" he asked then, but I knew it was an afterthought. An hour or so would be spent remembering, and I would be the outsider to whom all hometown jokes would have to be explained.

"No, thanks, Tom. I'll just putter around here. I'll see you later." I hung up quickly before the tears in my throat could thicken my voice. I knew I was being irrational to resent Tom's taking old friends to lunch. Surely I could trust Tom's love. . . . *I'm just disappointed at not being able to see him as soon as I'd thought,* I told myself.

Suddenly, I wished I had taken him up on his invitation. I would have liked to meet his lost Eleanor. Or would I? Perhaps the competition would be more than I could handle.

The throbbing in my head was worse. I went into the bathroom and got two Bufferin and a paper cup of water, noting as I swallowed them that they were the last two in the bottle. I had suffered from so many headaches lately. I would have to buy more or ask Tom to bring some home, for the headaches would probably continue until the humidity dropped.

I went into the bedroom and lay down across the unmade bed, willing myself to relax, hoping to sleep away the pain and my jealousy of Tom and Eleanor.

Around ten, I awoke to the sound of a steady rain on the roof and windowpanes. I stretched, luxuriating in the soothing, almost musical drumming, and prepared to doze off again. But somehow the rain, though fairly gentle, was not making me feel sleepy. My head hurt a bit less, but I could feel tension tightening my muscles and stiffening my spine.

" 'Methought I heard a voice cry, "Sleep no more! Macbeth doth murder sleep," ' " I intoned dramatically, thinking of Mr. Rob. But somehow it wasn't funny, and I shivered.

I got up and went into the living room, grabbed Tom's reference Bible from the bookshelf, and brought it back to bed with me. Thinking of Mr. Rob reminded me of the ghost stories he had said the Bible contained.

Quickly, I ran my finger down the columns of the "Biblical Cyclopedic Index" in the front of the book, stopping at the word *ghost*. It was explained as "soul or spirit," and two references were listed: "Surrender of, signifies death . . . Gen. 35:29 and Mark 15:37."

I turned to Genesis and read: "And Isaac gave up the ghost, and died, and was gathered unto his people, being old and full of days: and his sons Esau and Jacob buried him."

Some ghost story! I thought. I turned to Mark. The passage read: "And Jesus cried with a loud voice, and gave up the ghost."

Well, I thought, *so much for biblical ghosts.* I couldn't see that either verse had much to do with Lucretia haunting my valley, but perhaps Mr. Rob was more familiar with the Bible than I was. He had quoted a verse from Matthew that wasn't listed here. *Sometime,* I promised myself, *I'm going to ask him which passages he meant when he said the Bible is full of ghost stories.*

I reached out to lay the Bible on the antique walnut washstand I used for a bedside table, and saw an envelope flutter from its pages to the floor. I leaned over the edge of the bed and picked it up. It was addressed to Tom at the Lexington office and had been forwarded to him at his new office here. It was marked **Personal**.

Probably some correspondence about a legal matter he's handling, I thought. Then as I started to replace it in the Bible, the return address leaped out at me. It was from the welfare office that had supervised my passing from home to home during my childhood.

Without hesitation, I removed the single page from the envelope and unfolded it. It was dated a couple of days earlier, and I gasped in shock and pain as I read:

> *Dear Mr. Farris:*
>
> *In answer to your inquiry concerning the history of Amanda Teague, I am happy to inform you that we know of no mental illness on either side of her family.*
>
> *I feel it only fair to add, however, that we know little about her maternal ancestry except that her grandparents died many years ago and her mother was an only child. Our extensive investigations have turned up nothing to indicate. . . .*

The page blurred before my eyes, and I sank back onto the pillow, numb with the loss of faith I once had had in our mutual love and trust. To think that Tom, behind my back, had cold-bloodedly inquired into my past, as though I were a company seeking merger with one of his corporations, and had requested the letter sent to his office where no telling who had read it, in spite of the **Personal** notation! I wouldn't have believed it if I hadn't held the black-and-white proof in my hands. It was such an utter betrayal of all I felt for him, of our love which had seemed so precious these past months.

I was crying now from hurt and anger. If I couldn't love Tom wholeheartedly, without reservation, and if I couldn't trust his love, then I was completely alone, as I had been all my life. It was a bleak, empty feeling, much worse than never knowing love at all.

When the storm of tears had passed, I lay on the bed exhausted and desolate. My head hurt, and my eyes were sore and swollen. Eventually I slept, but only to drift in and out of troubled dreams. . . .

. . . I saw Tom at a distance holding hands with a beautiful woman. I was crying loudly, holding out empty hands to their retreating backs. Daren Blake came toward me, winking his dark eyes and mocking my tears with his laughter. . . .

. . . The laughter faded from the dark eyes, and they became haunted with despair. I was crying quietly, heartbroken. My hands clung to him. Then Joel tore himself from my arms and was running into the woods, and my grief was too deep for tears. . . .

. . . I was driving Annabel, and the house with the white rose was beckoning me to it. I left the car and went inside. The door slammed behind me, and I turned in fright and jerked at the knob, but the door would not open. A voice whispered, *"You are mine."* My bruised, empty heart felt such empathy with the voice that I had no power to resist. *"You are mine!"* the voice shouted jubilantly. . . .

I awakened as weird, demonic laughter escaped from my throat.

SEVENTEEN

I threw back the cover, glad to be out of the nightmares at last. My head still ached as I smoothed the blue and yellow spread over the bed and dressed slowly in green wool slacks and a matching sweater. I slipped my feet into loafers and went into the kitchen.

Things seemed familiar and yet strangely out of place. I walked through the house, straightening, rearranging. My head throbbed dully and my movements were slow and lethargic.

The creek was roaring again. Or was it my head? I couldn't think clearly. Suddenly, I had to get away. I grabbed my purse and left the house. I had no idea where I was going, but there seemed to be something I needed to do. The drugstore came into my thoughts and hung there.

I knew it was too far to walk, but somehow I was reluctant to get into the car. I had the disoriented feeling of standing back watching myself. I shook my head to clear it, got the key into the ignition, and started the car. It lurched crazily down the driveway, but driving down the winding country road helped clear my thoughts.

I felt more like myself now and I knew what I wanted to do. I would go shopping for material to make those draperies I had promised Tom for his new office. Perhaps, as shopping usually did, it would cheer me up. I couldn't remember what had depressed me in the first place, except for the headache and the gloomy weather.

When I saw Chad walking along the side of the road, I hit my brakes to stop; but he threw me one glance, then disappeared over the roadbank so quickly it was hard to believe he had been there at all. It was Saturday so school was out. He had every right to be out walking along the road if he so desired. He had been perfectly willing to ride the last time I had stopped for him. Then I remembered how frightened he had been the day he had made the compost and I had called him Tarrellton. I guessed he was still afraid of me. That hurt, for I wanted so badly to be his friend.

I parked Annabel at the edge of the square, which was busier than it usually was on weekdays, and walked around the courthouse looking for a store that sold fabrics.

Across the street from the back of the courthouse, I found what I was seeking—a small fabric shop that handled nothing but sewing materials. I entered the shop, and a short, plump, middle-aged blonde graciously asked if she could help me.

"I'd like to look around first, if I may," I told her.

She nodded and smiled and went back to arranging some yarns in the store window.

I chose a bright-patterned drapery cloth for Tom's office. Then I found myself fingering some beautiful upholstery material, thinking of the chairs and sofa in his waiting room that badly needed recovering.

What am I thinking of? I wondered suddenly. Very simple clothing and curtains were the extent of my sewing abilities. I wouldn't dare tackle the easiest slipcover job, much less try to upholster an office full of old furniture that would, no doubt, need the springs rebuilt and other drastic surgery about which I knew nothing.

I moved on to the bonded woolens. Some of the colors and textures were simply beautiful. I couldn't keep my hands off them. Though I usually refused to buy the expensive bonded wool for fear of ruining it and wasting my money, today I simply couldn't resist a misty blue heather plaid. The end of the bolt said "Made in Scotland." I visualized it made up in a skirt that fit snugly over the hips and flared into swinging pleats around my legs. I was slim enough for plaids and pleats, but I had never made anything with pleats. An A-line or simple gore was my speed. Of course, the plaids would have to be matched, too. Somehow, though, today I had confidence in my ability to make that misty plaid into just the skirt I pictured.

I found a pattern that could be altered to suit my idea. Impulsively, I asked for the needed amount of material, selected a zipper and matching thread, then paid in cash. Leaving the store, I wondered where I could find a bulky knit sweater of that same shade of blue.

Half an hour later, I was back in front of the fabric shop still wondering. No sweater anywhere in town matched my material.

Oh, well, I thought, shifting my heavy package from one arm to the other, *maybe when we get a chance to run over to Lexington. . . .* But the enticing display of yarns and knitting needles in the window caught my eye. I took out the woolen material I had bought and, yes, one of the yarns was the perfect match! It would take longer, but a hand-knitted sweater would be perfect with the wool. I could almost feel its warmth against my skin and visualize the lovely blue turning my green eyes almost the same shade.

I had gone inside the shop, had asked for all the heather blue yarn in stock plus knitting needles, and was making out a check before I remembered that I didn't know how to knit! One of my foster mothers had tried to teach me to knit and crochet, but I hadn't been able to learn to do even a simple chain stitch. Whatever had possessed me to ask for all that yarn?

"You're new in town, aren't you?" the clerk was saying. "I'll be glad to take your check, ma'am, but I'll have to see some identification."

I nodded absently. I was ashamed to ask her to take back the yarn. I could just hear myself saying, "Lady, I'm sorry, but the truth is I don't know how to knit and I don't even intend to learn!" *It'll be all over town that Tom Farris' wife bought an armful of yarn that she couldn't possibly use in a hundred years,* I thought.

The clerk was staring at the name printed across the top of my check. Then she stared at me with a strange, almost sickly look. *Another of Tom's hometown fans,* I thought. I would keep the yarn if I had to tie packages with it for forty Christmases to come!

Smiling brightly at her, I handed her the check and my driver's license, but she shook her head.

"That's all right, Mrs. Farris," she said softly. "I . . . know your husband."

I thanked her and hurried out with my arms full of material and many skeins of yarn I likely would never use. I didn't even have anybody on my Christmas list to whom I could give it. I was stuck with it.

Whatever made me do such a stupid thing? I wondered crossly. I could have used the money for so many things!

My head was beginning to ache again. I was on the street behind the courthouse, but it all looked different. The town seemed to have shrunk and faded like a much-washed dress, and there were vacant lots between the buildings that I had never noticed before.

In the back of my mind, there seemed to be something I had to do, some special reason I had come to town. I tried to remember what it was as I automatically took a shortcut across the courthouse lawn to the other side of the square.

Then I remembered. It was the drugstore I had wanted to visit today. I hurried across to it, then stopped in the doorway. But what was it I had wanted?

The store was dim inside. It was such a gloomy day, and my thoughts were a perfect match, as perfect as the yarn was for the wool I had bought. . . .

. . . Why did I do such a foolish, impulsive thing?

I chided myself. I could finish the sweater in no time, but it was getting too cold for just a sweater. I fingered the wool in its paper bag. It was so pretty, but it was neither the proper color nor the proper thickness for a boy's winter coat.

"What do you want?" A white-haired man, wearing a white shirt with black sleeve garters, stood behind the long wooden counter under the Apothecary *sign.*

"Laudanum," I whispered, hoping he would see his way clear to put this one last item on my long overdue account. I needed the tincture of opium.

"I want a large bottle of laudanum, please," I repeated, louder this time.

The old man stared at me, his eyes as cold as gray stone. I felt sure he was going to refuse me. Frantically, I searched my mind for a way to convince him that I must have it. But he turned and went toward the back of the store without comment. I waited, nervously twisting my fingers together.

"May I help you, lovely lady?"

The loud voice cut through my throbbing head. I put up one hand and pressed my temple. My head and limbs felt heavy, and my movements felt similar to swimming under water. I tried to focus on the bright dark eyes in the smiling face behind the gleaming glass counter. Wooden counter? Glass?

Whatever it was, I caught at it with one hand as I swayed.

"Hey, are you all right?" A voice boomed. He's coming around the counter! I must get what I came for, *I thought in panic,* and get away from here!

"Laudanum," I gasped, warding him off with my hands.

"Laudanum?" The voice rose incredulously. "Did you say, 'laudanum'?"

I nodded. "Mr. . . . ," but the name eluded me. "The old man—he went to get it."

"What?" He stared at me. "Amanda, what's wrong? There's no one here but me. I was in the back alone when you came in. I thought you looked. . . . Here, sit down."

I turned and ran. I glanced back from the edge of the square. The man stood in the doorway watching me with a puzzled frown. I didn't slow down again until I had put the town behind me and was pounding full speed down the dusty road.

E I G H T E E N

*Looking back to make sure no one was following me,
I stopped to catch my breath, clutching the fierce
pain that suddenly knifed my side. "There's no need
to run. I've got plenty of time." I started down the
road at a walk.*

*My package was getting heavier, reminding me of
the foolish purchases I had made.* Oh, well, *I thought,*
it's done now. The wool's been cut from the bolt, and
I've paid for it. I can't do anything about it. It'll make
Susannah a nice warm dress. Maybe I can do some
sewing now that Christmas is near. Maybe I can knit
and sell the blue sweater. If I can earn enough to
buy material for Tarrellton's coat and to get something for Harrison, perhaps I can get them all done
in time for Christmas.

*I hated thinking about Christmas without Joel,
but I'd have to do something for the children. The
boys would understand why we were having the*

usual Christmas dinner with Grandma and Grandpa Adams, but not having our own overladen table on Christmas Eve. Susannah wouldn't care much about the supper, anyway. I could make her china doll a new rag body with a dress of the blue plaid to match her own. Of course, she would still expect an orange and a candy cane from St. Nicholas.

I was amazed to see the church ahead. Had I come over two miles already? I could feel the hate boiling up inside me, smothering out thoughts of Christmas and the children.

Impulsively, I turned toward the white building with its cross over the door. The hinges squeaked as I pushed the door open and went inside. Here, every Sunday, the good people of the community met to sing and pray and sit in pious complacency as their pastor verbally patted them on the head for being such good children.

How I hated that bunch of sanctified hypocrites! In their minds they had tried and convicted Joel without a thought of mercy or even justice! Their precious hallowed ground was too good for the likes of him, they had decided. How I hated them! Not one of them was fit to polish Joel's boots!

I went slowly down the aisle, touching the brass nameplates on the pews, thinking of their owners.

Hawkins. Silas and Dora Hawkins, both of them so stingy they turned their hogs loose to fatten on other people's crops.

"He's a deserter!" Dora had said. "He ain't got no right to rest amongst decent folks!" I struck the Hawkins' nameplate with my fist and moved on to the next pew.

Smith. William and Martha, a tall, spare couple with five sober-faced daughters and four rebellious sons. They were so straight-laced they wouldn't allow the children to laugh on Sundays and kept them so overburdened with work on weekdays that they had no time or energy for merriment.

"He's committed the unpardonable sin!" William Smith had told them all at their secret meeting. "No suicide ought to be buried in hallowed ground."

Who was William Smith to decide what was the unpardonable sin? And, anyway, Joel hadn't committed it. My fist fell on the Smith nameplate and I moved on.

Watkins. Sam and Esther, a young couple so wrapped up in each other they probably didn't even know Joel had died. I passed that pew. They were newlyweds; they could be excused.

Across the aisle was the name Miller. Sophie was the only one left in that pew now, since Ed had been killed at Perryville and Eddie now rode with Morgan's raiders. I could still see the contempt in her eyes as she had viewed Joel in his coffin and then had turned to offer me false condolences. I struck her nameplate and moved toward the Luther pew.

I had nothing against Jed, who spent Sunday mornings in that pew sleeping off the aftereffects of Saturday night. It was that Nellie Luther's sharp tongue that had cut Joel's character to shreds, in spite of the fact that her own husband was shiftless and ornery, or maybe because of it. How dared she even hold Joel's name in her vile mouth? My fist condemned Nellie Luther.

I continued down the aisle, condemning first one

side, then the other, skipping a pew now and then.
Few of this congregation were innocent of Joel's final
humiliation—the Lafontaines, the Adamses, a half
dozen, no more. These innocent might have to suffer
with the guilty, but who had suffered more unjustly
than the children and I? Than Joel? For though Joel
had left his company, he was as innocent of taking
his own life as any man in this church.

I heard footsteps on the path outside. It must be
later than I thought. Already, they were coming back
for the night service. I slipped behind one of the big
double doors, knowing that when it was open it
would hide me. Then, as they passed down the aisle,
I could slip out and do what I now knew I must do
to avenge Joel.

The door swung back and I could not be seen, but
neither could I see them as they filed into their pews.
Finally, though, the footsteps on the bare wooden
floor stopped. I crept from behind the door. In the
dimness, I could see only one small boy rummaging
in the closet near the pulpit, but I knew they were
all in their brass-marked pews.

I slipped outside into the gathering twilight. I
couldn't move to the front of the church now to get
what I needed, but if I hurried, I could go home and
get the necessary things and be back before the service was over.

I heard a roar and a screech behind me, followed
by the sound of running feet. I turned quickly and
saw a very big and very blond man with blue eyes
that were troubled under his frown. I didn't like him,
but I wasn't afraid of him, and I wasn't answering

any of his stupid questions. It was none of his concern whether or not I was all right!

He forced me into a big gray machine, and we hurtled down the road at tremendous speed.

"What's wrong with Annabel?" he asked suddenly.

Did he mean Susannah? Then I knew who he must be. (If only my thoughts didn't seem so much like square pegs in round holes!) He was that horrible traveling salesman Lucy Lafontaine had introduced to me. He had wasted no time in telling me he wanted to marry me and take me West with him.

I felt hate rise in me again. There never would be any man for me but Joel, even though he was buried in the woods, thanks to the people of the church.

My thoughts swung back to the congregation. Fools! All of them! Especially that fanatical captain who had shot Joel without a trial and then had said Joel grabbed the gun and shot himself to keep from going back. "He was on his way back!" I said aloud.

"What, sweetheart?" the blond man asked.

Sweetheart? He took a lot for granted. But I didn't say anything. He was turning the machine into our lane. When we got to the house, I would simply demand that he leave. If he persisted in forcing his unwanted attentions on me, there was Joel's rifle, the one they had given back to me for Harrison. I wouldn't be bothered by this obnoxious giant for long!

As we entered the house, I glanced into the parlor at the gun cabinet and saw with relief that Joel's rifle was there, ready. I kept a shell in it, ready to fire, for I knew if I needed it in a hurry, I never would get it loaded in time. But because of the children, I kept the gun cabinet locked. My thoughts swirled through my aching head. The key was in a vase on the mantel. If I—

"Now, sweetheart. . . ." He reached for me with his hateful hands. I fluttered my eyelashes at him, winningly, I hoped, and eased out of his embrace. "I wonder if you'd mind gettin' a little kindlin' to start a fire in the range so I can make us some coffee?" I asked. His eyes widened, but I smiled brightly and pushed him toward the kitchen. Then I clutched my skirts and ran on tiptoe into the parlor. I grabbed the vase and spilled its contents into my hand. There was no key!

I raced to the gun cabinet and pulled frantically at the latch. It swung open, and I leaned against it weakly. Then, hearing his step on that squeaky board in the hall, I snatched the rifle from its supports and hid it behind me as I stepped away from the cabinet and moved behind the wing chair.

He came through the doorway, and I saw his eyes go immediately to the cabinet and take in the empty space and the telltale swinging door. His eyes flicked back to me.

"Amanda?"

A bitter smile touched my lips. He called Susannah "Annabel," and now he couldn't even remember my name! But I didn't care what he called me so long as he kept his hateful hands off me.

"Get out of this house!" I ordered quietly, raising the gun in front of me and steadying it across the chair back.

Shock registered in his eyes and spilled over his face. "Sweetheart! What is this?" He started toward *me, but I motioned him back with the gun barrel. His face was a mask of disbelief. His hands moved helplessly at his sides as he stared at me in growing horror.*

"Amanda? O God!" His moan matched the horror on his face and sent chills down my spine, but I wasn't going to start feeling sorry for him.

He wiped the horror from his face with one hand and came toward me, holding out his hand. "Give me the gun, Amanda."

"I told you to get out of here!" I hissed. "Joel's dead and buried, but you ain't fit to—"

"Amanda, you don't know what you're saying!"

Suddenly there was a knock on the front door. I froze. Was it the children? I couldn't shoot a man right before their eyes! They had lived through enough as it was.

"Tom! It's Daren!" a voice called. "Is everything OK?"

My head hurt so! If only I could think! I lowered the gun as I pressed the fingers of one hand against my throbbing temple.

He moved toward me, and I raised the gun again to point at his chest.

Could I actually shoot a man? Could I aim this rifle, pull the trigger, and watch him fall on my parlor floor to writhe in agony and blood?

My head! My thoughts were like nails driven through it. I couldn't shoot a man. . . . But I had killed before, hadn't I? I had taken the children by the hand. . . . No! No! The children were alive. Perhaps they stood now outside the door, waiting.

I felt his strong arms go around me. How I hated

*him! No man had ever held me in his arms but Joel.
No man ever would. I struggled to raise the rifle, to
aim it at some vital part of his body.*

*He was so much bigger than I, but my hate and
fear gave me added strength. I fought him like a
cornered cat, hissing and kicking and trying to bite
as he pulled me from behind the chair.*

*The door crashed behind us as it flew open. Then
a second pair of hands were holding my upper arms
from behind, pinning them to my sides. I had the
gun barrel pointing straight up between us. I pushed
it toward his face with all my strength, closed my
eyes, and squeezed the trigger.*

*Instead of the deadly crack of sound I had expected,
there was a hollow, empty click. The rifle was torn
from my hands. The only sound in the room was
panting, ragged breathing.*

*Then the pain in my head began turning black
and spreading over my body. . . .*

NINETEEN

"Tom, listen to me!" The voice cut through the peaceful darkness where I drifted, but the voice murmuring in my ear was soft and soothing. I let myself drift.

"Tom, you gotta do something!" I moaned a soft protest as the loud voice cut through the darkness again. "Man, she tried to kill you!"

It was raining. I could feel the warm drops on my face. When I touched the wetness with my tongue, it was salty. I opened my eyes and looked up into blue eyes flooded with tears. I pushed myself up against his supporting arms. I knew who he was now. He was Amanda's husband. I had been so wrapped up in the past I hadn't recognized him.

The dark-eyed man from the drugstore leaned against the mantel. He straightened when he saw my eyes upon him. His face held some strong emotion—bewilderment, fear?

"Tom, you can't—," he began.

"I'll talk with you later, Daren," he answered quickly. There was a warning in his voice.

"Now, look here, Tom, I followed you out here because I was worried. She was acting strangely when she came out of Mrs. Hobson's shop. Then, when she came into the store, she was downright weird! It gave me goose bumps! That's when I called you—"

"I appreciate all you've done, Daren. I'll talk with you later," he repeated firmly. I struggled to turn around so I could see what was going on, but he held me close against his chest. I heard footsteps. Then the door closed with a small but definite bang. Seconds later, I heard a roaring down the lane.

He lifted me from the floor, carried me into a bedroom, and deposited me on top of a blue and yellow spread. He held me by the arms as he leaned over me, forcing me to look at him as he spoke.

"Amanda, I'm calling a doctor. I want you to lie here quietly until I get back."

I was too drained of energy to do anything else. He was speaking softly to someone in the hallway. I couldn't distinguish what he was saying.

He came back into the room and stood looking at me for a moment, his blue eyes deeply troubled. I wasn't sure what was going on now, but I was too tired to care. I lay limply, watching him put nightgowns, a robe and slippers, and various cosmetics into a small suitcase.

He picked up the Bible beside the bed, looked at the letter on top of it, then quickly at me. I closed my eyes, pretending to sleep. When I opened them, he was closing the latch on the suitcase.

"Sweetheart," he said as he helped me up from

the bed and smoothed my hair, "I'm taking you where you can get help. . . ." His voice broke. I was still too exhausted to care where he took me. He caught me to him and held me as though he would never let me go. "Trust me, baby!" he begged. "You're going to be all right. I . . . I promise."

I went with him quietly. I simply didn't have the strength to oppose him. I was so desperately tired and still more than a little confused. I needed time. I closed my eyes. When I opened them again, we were parked in front of a small white brick building.

He got out, took the suitcase from the back, and came around to help me. It seemed easier to quietly obey whatever he told me to do.

He sat me in a chair inside the wide glass doors and set the case beside me. I waited docilely while he spoke to a woman behind the counter. After a while, he came back and led me down a long corridor and into a green-walled room with a high bed, a table, two chairs, and flowered curtains. Then I noticed the iron bars across the window, and my heart sank. It wasn't going to be as easy as I had thought. I would be a prisoner here. If only I could think! My head felt heavy, wooden. I had so much yet to do!

A nurse came in and helped me to undress and put on one of the gowns from the suitcase. The nightgown was a little wrinkled where he had laid the Bible on it, and it left me indecently bare in places, but it was a good fit. The nurse smiled at me, laid the Bible on the table, helped me into bed, and left.

He came back in then, and I pulled the thin cover up over my nakedness.

"Are you cold, sweetheart?" He spread a blanket from the foot of the bed up over me, kissed me on the forehead, and said he would see me later. His eyes were dark with misery as he left.

It was quiet in the room, and I could feel myself beginning to relax. I let my weary bones sink into the mattress. It was good to rest for now. I'd have time later for the things I must do. I was so tired.

The opening of the door awakened me from a deep, dreamless sleep.

"Mrs. Farris?" a voice inquired pleasantly. He was young, small, and dark with a trim mustache.

"No, I'm not Mrs. Farris," I answered.

"Oh?" He raised his dark eyebrows questioningly. "You're not Amanda Farris, wife of one of the greatest forwards in UK basketball history?"

I shook my head, but I couldn't help responding to his infectious smile.

He examined a folder in his hand, then stepped back and inspected the number on the outside of the door. "Now, Mrs. Farris," he scolded teasingly as he came toward the bed, "you are playing games with me! I'm Dr. Revel. Your husband tells me you've been a little upset lately. Suppose you tell me what it is that troubles you, and perhaps we can—"

He was testing me, treating me like a child, and not a very bright one at that. I could see I wasn't going to get anywhere by being nice.

"My husband is dead," I interrupted coldly.

His sad-looking brown eyes were keenly interested. "Your husband is dead," he repeated. It was a statement, not a question. "All right, Mrs. Farris. . . ."

My head was beginning to hurt again. A wave of

confusion swept over me like fog, then cleared. "I'm not Mrs. Farris!" I snapped.

He studied me. "I see," he said finally. "All right. Would you care to tell me who you are?"

"My name is Lucretia Adams."

"Lucretia Adams," he repeated, writing in the folder. "Very well, Lucretia. Now, what is bothering you so?"

Suddenly, I was fed up with his stupidity. "My husband was shot as a deserter by a captain from his own army and branded a suicide. He was neither. He was refused burial in the church graveyard and lies in a slave graveyard in the woods. My three children shrivel daily before my eyes. A strange man comes into my home and wants . . . well, whatever he wanted, and when I resist him, he bundles me off to a barred room where I am kept a prisoner and asked idiotic questions and called by the wrong name, and you ask what is bothering me?"

I could hear the ugly screech my voice had become, but he merely watched me with glittering eyes, as fascinated by me as a small boy prodding a toad with a stick. I turned my back on him and drew the covers up over my head.

"Excuse me, Mrs. . . . uh, Lucretia," he murmured. "I'll be right back." I heard the door shut behind him.

I glanced at the barred window. The sky was pitch black except where lamps on posts threw a glow against it. I must have slept longer than I had realized.

Perhaps it would be best if I waited until morning to try to get away from here. The children would be *safe with Ma and Pa Adams, and I would need daylight to get my bearings. I had no idea where this building was. Surely, though, we hadn't come far to reach it.*

"Lucretia?" The doctor's glittery eyes watched me expectantly from the door. "I've brought someone to see you."

I said nothing, but he came in anyway, followed by an older man. The eyes of the short, gray, rumpled-looking man were paler than Dr. Revel's, but they watched me just as keenly.

"This is Dr. Platner, Lucretia," Dr. Revel said. "I'd like you to tell him what you told me a few moments ago." I stared at him mutely. "You know," he prompted, "about your husband and the children."

Dr. Platner continued to watch me for several seconds, then turned to the younger doctor. "Suppose you leave us alone," he suggested quietly. Dr. Revel's eyes clouded with disappointment, but he obeyed the order without question.

"If you don't feel like talking, my dear," Dr. Platner said when we were alone, "I can come back some other time. Is there anything you need?" I shook my head no. "Your husband will be back tomorrow, Mrs. Farris, and—"

"My husband is dead!" I shouted then. "I am Lucretia Adams, and my husband is dead and buried!"

"I see," he said slowly, echoing Dr. Revel.

"Do you?" I challenged bitterly. "Then why don't you let me go home to my children?"

"Now, now, my dear. Don't get upset. I'm sure the . . . uh . . . children are fine."

He left the room briefly and came back with a long needle. Before I could protest, he stuck it ex-

pertly into my arm. "You rest now, and we will talk again tomorrow." He withdrew the needle, swabbed the puncture with wet cotton, and patted me reassuringly. The last thing I remember was the door closing behind him as he tiptoed from the room.

When I awoke, a faint sunlight was beginning to come through the window. At first I was puzzled by the black stripes it threw across the bed. Then it all came back—the barred window, the doctors, everything.

I had to get out of here! I had some extremely important things to do. Then I might be willing to see who was the stronger—the doctors or me, but then it wouldn't matter.

I got up quickly, found some clothes in the closet, and pulled them on. They weren't mine, but the green trousers and sweater fit me well, and I supposed a man's trousers might help to disguise me from a distance.

I took the suitcase from under the bed, got out a comb, and pinned up my hair. Leaving the suitcase behind, I pulled open the door and peered around it into the corridor. It was silent and deserted except for one nurse who sat behind a counter about halfway down the hall. She was writing. How could I get by her without being noticed? There had to be a way!

As I watched, a red light beside the nurse began to flash. She said something into a box in the wall, and a voice answered her. She was up and leaving her post! She was coming this way! Quickly, I shut the door and held my breath until I heard her whispery footsteps pass in the hall outside.

When I dared peep out again, the long hall was

empty. I slipped into it and walked quickly but quietly toward the opposite end from where the nurse had disappeared. I could hear a moaning from down that way, and a muffled sobbing came from behind one of the closed doors I passed, but I had no time to borrow trouble.

Just ahead were the big double glass doors that shut this corridor off from the one it crossed. I went through them and stopped, breathing deeply of the disinfectant-scented air. My heart pounded in my chest. So far, I had seen no one. But which way was the entrance—left or right? I tried to remember which way we had turned when we had come. I thought it was left. I turned right and followed the corridor around a corner. In front of me were the double glass doors.

The sun shone brightly through the heavy glass, my gateway to freedom! I wanted to run, but I knew that would only arouse the suspicions of the girl behind the glass-enclosed counter. I forced myself to walk, agonizingly slowly, toward the doors. Then I was through them, and the girl hadn't even looked up. Only the steps and the lawn lay between me and the road.

A man was crossing the lawn from the parking area. He seemed to be looking straight at me. I turned my head a little to the side and started down the steps. From the corner of my eye, I could see that he still watched me. He came closer then suddenly began to run.

I jumped the remaining steps and fell onto the grass. I was up and running toward the road, but he was fast and my fall had given him the advantage.

He grabbed me by both arms before I was halfway across the lawn. I struggled with him, but he expertly turned my arm behind my back and the pain when I struggled forced me to be still.

"Now, Mrs. Farris, that's better," Dr. Revel panted. "Where did you think you were going so early this morning without even saying good-bye? Back home to shoot your husband?"

I glared at him, but he laughed. "Don't tell me! I know. Your husband was killed in the Civil War." Then his attitude changed from mockery to concern. "I'm sorry," he apologized, bringing my arm back to my side. He held it firmly just above the elbow as he guided me back across the lawn and into the white building.

"You let this one get away, Robbie," he called to the nurse, who was back at her desk busily writing.

She looked up, gasped, and jumped up to follow us into that same barred room I had left only moments before.

"Now, Mrs. Farris, we want to help you," Dr. Revel said when we were in the room. He shut the door and leaned against it while the nurse hunted for my gown and slippers. "This is, essentially, a regular hospital with a small psychiatric ward," he explained, "but if you insist on giving us trouble, we can have you transferred to a mental facility."

He beckoned to the nurse, who handed me my gown and followed him outside. I kicked off my shoes and ran barefoot to the door to listen to what they were saying. His voice was low, but I heard the words "paranoid schizophrenia." I had no idea what they meant. Then in a more normal tone, he said, "As soon as her husband comes in, send him to my office."

I undressed and put on the gown. The nurse came back and took away the green trousers and sweater and shoes. I realized I would not be able to escape. But I had to get out!

My mind was functioning much more clearly than it had yesterday. I supposed it was just a matter of getting used to it.

I had tried others, but none of them ever really understood. One fool had burned the house. This one had no family, except that stupid Tom who liked to shoot squirrels. Unless she joined them in fighting me. . . . But she wouldn't. My will was much stronger than hers, and she had no faith. Rarely, when I wanted to come to her, had she been able to resist me. The story I had so carefully shown her had done its work. She had such sympathy for me! I laughed mockingly.

That hateful Tom was different altogether. His faith was strong. I couldn't touch him, except through Amanda. I would need help with him, I admitted. But he loved this silly Amanda. If only I could. . . .

All at once, I knew what I had to do to get out, to accomplish all the things I needed to do, and to destroy that blond giant I hated so. I wasn't afraid to risk it. I was confident I could take control whenever I desired. For now, though, retreat was the only weapon I had. . . .

TWENTY

. . . My first thought was that I had been asleep. *It must have been a dream!* I thought, relieved to be awake. When I saw the bars on the window, I screamed.

"Mrs. Farris, what is going on in here?" The nurse's tone showed annoyance.

"What is this place? What am I doing here? Where's my husband?" My voice touched on hysteria as the questions tumbled out.

"I'd better get the doctor," she said, backing out of the room without answering any of my questions.

The doctor stopped just inside the door and looked at me. He was young, dark, and neat, and he had a sarcastic smile. "Well, well, how are we now?" he asked. "Or maybe I should say, *who* are we now?"

I looked at him in genuine puzzlement. "I am Amanda Farris. Where is my husband? Why can't I see him?"

His dark eyebrows rose. "Oh, you may see him, Mrs. Farris, if you want to."

"What do you mean? Of course I want to see him!"

He shrugged. "The last time I mentioned him, you informed me that he had been dead for a hundred years."

"Don't be ridiculous. . . ." Then I was remembering. It still seemed like something I had dreamed. I couldn't really have done all the crazy things that came into my memory like scenes from an old movie I had seen years ago! But I did seem to remember screaming at the doctor that my husband was dead and that my name was. . . . "O God!" I moaned. "What am I going to do?"

I could see no sympathy in his eyes, merely a clinical interest. "Right now, Mrs. Farris, we're going to run some tests. Then Dr. Platner wants to talk with you. And if you are a good little girl, you may see your husband."

I wanted to slap that sarcastic grin off his face. I had so many questions, and I was so frightened! But I also had a vague memory of his twisting my arm. So I submitted to a long session of tests for what seemed to be eye, muscle, and brain coordination. Then Dr. Revel took some blood from my arm and left.

After lunch, I was taken to Dr. Platner's office. I remembered him, too, from that same old movie. He sat behind his desk, gray and rumpled—from his sagging suit to his thinning hair—but his eyes were keen and penetrating. He asked probing questions in a gentle and sympathetic manner, and I found myself responding frankly. Before the session was over, I had told him all about Lucretia Adams, beginning with my first vision of the gray house and ending with the burial scene at the church. Everything after that seemed a jumble that could not possibly be real.

"Your story matches that told me by your husband, Mrs. Farris," he said gravely when I had finished, "as far as it goes. Do you remember trying to shoot him?" His gray eyes probed mine.

Suddenly, my memory cleared. I was in my living room behind the wing chair, and I had Tom's rifle in my hands. "Dr. Platner, what am I going to do?" I cried, as the full impact of memory swept over me.

"You remember it?" he repeated.

"I do now. Doctor, please tell me the truth. Am I insane?"

He shook his head. "I don't think so, Mrs. Farris. Dr. Revel has the idea that you suffer from paranoid schizophrenia."

"Split personality?" I whispered in horror.

"Don't worry. There is a very simple test which we did just after Dr. Revel left you this morning. I fed some of your blood to a spider. Had you been a true schizophrenic, the spider would have immediately reacted to a chemical in your blood and would have begun to exhibit tendencies of schizophrenia. I'm happy to say your spider showed none of the usual symptoms. Therefore, I am inclined to rule out schizophrenia, though we have some other tests I want to make."

It sounded so bizarre that I wondered briefly if I had wandered into some Alice-in-Wonderland place where mad doctors went around feeding blood to spiders and doctoring their patients accordingly. I had to laugh. He looked at me quizzically.

"Your spider test sounds as crazy as my visits from Lucretia Adams," I explained.

He smiled. "A very thin line sometimes separates the so-called normal from the mentally disturbed. However, the spider test—like the frog or rabbit test for pregnancy—is as accurate as many more complicated procedures—"

"Do you have any idea what *is* wrong with me?" I broke in.

He got up from behind his desk, walked over to the window, and stood looking out. Finally, he turned to me. "Mental disorders fall into two classes, Mrs. Farris: the neurotic and the psychotic. The former reflects an environment hostile to one's nature, or is due to the stress of living or to some chemical imbalance in the body. I have come to believe that with the latter, more often than any of us realize, the victim is the host of some troubled discarnate who has attached himself to the mind of his victim like a parasite. I believe that many suicides of drug addicts, months after they have stopped using any drugs or hallucinogens, are due to the fact that the drugged mind is especially susceptible to possession, which cannot be ended simply by ceasing to take drugs."

I stared at him, fascinated. I had dreaded seeing a psychiatrist, yet he was the first person I had found who believed what I thought had been happening to me was possible.

"In plain English, doctor, you're saying that it's possible that the spirit of someone named Lucretia Adams could be trying to take over my body, could be influencing me to see and do things?"

"Mrs. Farris, I simply do not know. I believe the soul is an electromagnetic force that, even though the body dies, can never be destroyed. This psychic-energy force separates from the physical body at death and enters a new existence on the spiritual level. Sometimes, if the disembodied spirit is troubled, it will seek to attach itself to another living human body in order to return to the physical world to achieve some goal—vengeance or the solving of some problem left unresolved at an untimely death—"

"You say, '*I* believe,'" I interrupted. "Does this mean that Dr. Revel does not share your belief?"

He laughed. "That's putting it politely! Dr. Revel even goes so far as to say that when the Bible speaks of Jesus casting out demons, he simply was healing schizophrenics. I, however, feel that there was more to it than that, or why did the swine plunge over the cliff and drown themselves in the sea?"

I shook my head. I wasn't all that familiar with the story.

"At any rate, I do not believe you have been hallucinating," he went on. "I believe you have been shown someone's memories, perhaps as an urging toward some action." He smiled. "However, most psychiatrists would think I am as mentally disturbed as Dr. Revel thinks you are."

"Do you think she's gone?" I asked hopefully. "Yesterday seems like a bad dream, but I feel perfectly normal now."

He wouldn't meet my eyes as he sat back down at the desk and began to play with a paper clip.

"You think she is waiting," I answered for him. I could see the years stretched out ahead of me, never knowing when I would be normal or when she would be in command of my body, making me do and say things I later would remember with remorse. I had felt such sympathy for her, had even encouraged her visits. Now, it all seemed so horrible! *I'd rather be dead than live like this.* My thought must have shown in my face.

"Now, now, Mrs. Farris," he soothed. "Sometimes the spirit leaves of its own free will when it has accomplished its mission. Perhaps your Lucretia will do so."

I remembered the story of the young girl who, supposedly, had left after bringing her murderer to justice. But what if Lucretia's purpose wasn't so noble?

"Doctor, yesterday she tried . . . I tried to kill Tom," I reminded him. "What if her purpose is to have me commit murder?"

He shrugged. "I doubt that any jury in America would believe your story. You'd either be considered insane or diabolical enough to invent such an excuse for your crime. However, I don't believe you would be morally responsible for actions carried out under her influence."

"Morally responsible?" I echoed. "Doctor, the point is, my husband—or whoever—would be dead!"

He nodded. "That's true." He sat studying the pyramid he was building with his fingers. "I doubt, though, that she could make you commit any act strongly contrary to your own moral beliefs and feelings." His eyes met mine reassuringly.

"Dr. Platner, it wasn't my fault the gun was empty," I said, remembering the hollow click of the rifle as I had pulled the trigger. "If there had been a shell in that gun, Tom would now be. . . ." I turned my mind from the hideous picture the thought conjured up.

He sat studying me for several seconds. "Perhaps

you had some anger or resentment toward your husband that helped her overcome your natural scruples against killing," he suggested. "I can't see why a spirit from a hundred years ago would want to harm your husband. What could she possibly have against him?"

I was remembering the feelings I had had about the letter and Tom's luncheon date with Eleanor Hobson, but to think I might actually have wanted to kill Tom myself was worse than believing it all had been Lucretia. I didn't mention any of this to the doctor.

"Is there anything you can do to help me?" I asked instead.

"Honestly, I don't know, Mrs. Farris. I've done quite a bit of reading on this subject. The world of the spirit is the new frontier of scientific research. Until these last few years, anything supernormal was considered superstition. But scientists are beginning to realize that just because something can't be seen, heard, smelled, tasted, or touched doesn't mean it doesn't exist.

"Scientifically speaking," he went on, "it might be interesting to give this spirit, who supposedly is trying to borrow your physical body, a chance to communicate with us. Under controlled conditions, of course. And who knows? Perhaps our accomplishment of some unfinished task might free her troubled spirit from its bondage to the physical world."

"If it would free *me* of *her,* I would do anything!" I vowed. "Short of murder."

He chuckled. "I remember reading of a case where the patient showed every tendency of schizophrenia with delusions of grandeur. He thought he was a Spanish pirate and, though he had never learned any foreign language, could speak a form of Spanish when under the influence of his other 'personality.' However, like you, he failed the spider test and others. Eventually, he seemed normal and was dismissed. He went home from the hospital and, a few days later, under some compulsion he didn't understand, dug up his backyard where he uncovered a rusty iron box filled with Spanish coins. He did some research and found that his alter ego had actually existed. When he traced his alter ego's descendants and gave them the coins, the man was never again troubled by his Spanish pirate. Perhaps your story will end as well, Mrs. Farris. Have you dug up the backyard lately?"

I laughed with him. "Dr. Platner, this controlled experiment you spoke of, would you do it here at the hospital?"

"If possible. It seems that Lucretia retreated soon after you entered the clinic. She may not like it here or may feel threatened, or she may feel that it is the wrong place to accomplish whatever it is she wants done. A spiritualist or medium might prove helpful. Or perhaps some drug. Whatever we try, Mrs. Farris, you understand it would have to be with your husband's approval?"

"Of course." Surely Tom would be willing to try anything that might help me.

About an hour after I'd returned to my room, Tom came in, stopped just inside the door, and stood looking at me out of troubled eyes.

"Tom!" I said, smiling and holding out my arms to him. I saw relief wash over his features as he came eagerly toward the bed.

"Feeling better, sweetheart? I've been worried sick about you! Dr. Platner says he—"

"Tom," I interrupted, "did he tell you what he thinks is wrong with me?"

His mouth became a hard, straight line. "Yes, he told me."

"He mentioned some drug or maybe even using a medium to contact . . . ," I began.

"Amanda, I think we should try someone more qualified. I brought you here because it was the closest place, but—"

"Tom, I'm ready to try anything that might end this nightmare! I think Dr. Platner is right. I've tried to tell you all along that I have been seeing actual scenes from the past. Dr. Platner puts it that someone is 'showing me memories.' Tom, Lucretia wants me to do something for her. If I could find out what it is and do it—"

"Don't be ridiculous!" he almost shouted. "I will not let Dr. Platner use you as a guinea pig in his weird psychic experiments!" He made a visible effort at self-control, but I could see a blue vein throbbing in his temple. "Amanda, don't you realize that any spirit that would be trying to possess you could only be evil?"

"Oh, Tom!" I protested. "She wasn't evil. She was embittered—an innocent victim of circumstances."

He took the hand I reached out to him and sat on the side of the bed. "Amanda," he said earnestly, "you've got to stop feeling sorry for . . . whatever it is that is troubling you. The Bible speaks of demon possession, and I think you have encouraged possession, if that's what it is, by feeling sympathy—"

"If Lucretia were one of your down-and-out skid-row bums," I interrupted, "you'd feel so sorry for her, you'd bring her home to rehabilitate! Who could help feeling sympathy for her?"

"She tried to make you kill me!" he said incredulously. "And you still feel sympathy for her? Amanda, Jesus never once suggested that anyone pity the demons he cast out."

"Dr. Revel says Jesus was healing schizophrenia, not actually casting out demons," I challenged. Then I dropped my gaze to the bed. I knew I wasn't capable of arguing Scripture with Tom.

He got up and began pacing the room, counting facts off on his fingers. "Jesus was at the creation. Colossians 1 says so. John 1 says so," he pointed out in that now-ladies-and-gentlemen-let's-look-at-the-facts tone he used when he was being especially reasonable, charming, and convincing to a jury. "Do you think that he who created the human mind wouldn't have known the difference between a mental illness and demon possession? Except when he said he was telling a parable, Jesus spoke straight and plain. When he says he cast out a demon, there's no reason to believe he was doing anything else."

He paused and reached for the Bible on the nightstand. "Here, let me read you something from Luke." He flipped the pages expertly, ran his finger down a page, and began to read.

" 'When the evil spirit comes out of a man, it wanders through waterless places looking for rest, and when it fails to find any, it says, "I will go back to my house from which I came." When it arrives, it finds it cleaned and all in order. Then it goes and collects seven other spirits more evil than itself to keep it company, and they all go in and make themselves at home. The last state of that man is worse than the first.' That is demon possession, Amanda, no matter what Dr. Platner or Dr. Revel calls it."

A new and terrible thought hit me. "Tom, does that mean if we should find some way to 'cast out' Lucretia—or whatever is haunting me—I might then be susceptible to an even worse condition?"

He came back to the bed and took my hand again. "Sweetheart, if that man had filled his empty 'house' with the Spirit of God, there would have been no room for the evil spirits."

It all sounded like so much mumbo jumbo to me. "Hang a horseshoe upside down over your door and a witch will not enter your house!"

"Amanda." He leaned over me, his eyes boring into mine. "Let's call in a priest."

"A priest? But I'm not Catholic. Neither are you."

He shook his head impatiently. "No, but in this time and place, I don't know anyone else who might be familiar with the rites of exorcism."

Exorcism! The word knelled through my mind with the sound of doom. "Oh, Tom!" I tried to laugh, but it sounded shaky. "Maybe I'm being haunted, but I'm not possessed! Joel was a Christian. Maybe Lucretia, in her later years, became one, too. Maybe—"

"Amanda," Tom cut off my babbling, "dead Christians don't haunt. They go to be with the Lord. Believe me, whatever is bothering you is not Christian." He bent down and kissed me lightly. "I'll be back as soon as I find a priest who understands exorcism." At the door, he turned and looked back at me. "Trust me, sweetheart," he said. "It will be all right. I promise."

I watched the door close behind him. "Bring on your priest!" my voice said aloud to the empty room. Again, I wasn't sure the words were mine, but I knew one thing. I would resist an exorcism with all the powers at my command. I wasn't sure why.

TWENTY-ONE

About an hour after Tom left, there was a knock, and at my "Come in," a freckled face appeared around the door.

"A red-headed Irishman always pays his debts," Jimmy O'Brien said, holding out a thermos bottle in one hand and two Styrofoam cups in the other. He opened the thermos, poured two steaming cups of coffee, and handed one to me. "Hope you like it black."

I sipped it gingerly. "That's good!" I exclaimed.

Freckles slid into the crevices of his grin. "I told you Mrs. Baker makes a mean cup of coffee. And knowing hospital coffee, I thought now was a good time to bring you some."

"How did you know I was here, Reverend . . . uh, Brother . . . uh. . . ."

"Jimmy," he supplied. "My friends call me Jimmy. And Tom told me. He stopped by my office to ask about a priest." His blue eyes studied me seriously.

"That's quite a story he told me, Mrs. Farris!"

"My friends call me Amanda."

"Touché!" He grinned, and freckles disappeared again.

"Did you recommend one?" I asked warily.

He nodded. "I don't know if it's the right thing to do, but Tom was so set on it. . . ."

"I know."

"Mrs . . . Amanda, I'd like to hear your version, if you don't mind."

I took a deep breath. The first day I'd met Jimmy O'Brien, I had felt that I could tell him anything. I began with my first vision of the house and ended with my interview this afternoon with the doctor. "Dr. Platner thinks a medium might be helpful in finding out what she wants and—"

"Don't do it!" he warned. "No good can come from using the devil's tools. I once knew a minister who became a medium in 'a search for truth.' He died a hopeless alcoholic. I'd much rather see you try Tom's plan than that."

I sipped my coffee, avoiding his eyes.

"You don't want an exorcism, do you?" he probed.

Again, the word echoed through my mind with the sound of doom. "It just seems so . . . so. . . ."

"Out of the Dark Ages?" he suggested. I had been about to say "unfeeling," but I let it go. "Yes, it does," he continued, "but demon possession is a drastic condition that calls for drastic action."

"I just don't believe Lucretia is a demon."

"And I don't believe she's a ghost," he said. *"The Living Bible,* in Ecclesiastes 9, says that 'the dead know nothing; they don't even have their memories.

Whatever they did in their lifetimes—loving, hating, envying—is long gone, and they have no part in anything here on earth anymore.' "

"Someone once told me the Bible is full of ghost stories," I countered.

He frowned in concentration. "The only place I can think of where the Bible mentions dead people coming to life and walking around is in Matthew immediately after Jesus' resurrection when the graves were opened and many godly men and women arose and were seen by the people around Jerusalem. But, Amanda, that was a unique reaction to a unique event." He poured himself another cup of coffee and held the thermos out to me, but I shook my head. "Oh, yes," he added, "there was the incident where Saul had a medium call up the spirit of Samuel, but neither the Lord nor Samuel was too pleased about it."

"But is it possible, then, for us to reach the dead or, as in my case, for the dead to reach us?"

"Oh, I suppose it's possible, but it's not probable. You have to remember that this was not your average everyday happening."

I laughed. "How many people do you know who have had my recent experiences?"

He grinned. "Not many, I hope!" Concern replaced the grin on his face. "Amanda, why are you so opposed to exorcism?" His frank blue gaze challenged mine.

"I. . . ." But I couldn't explain it.

"Think about it!" he demanded. "The only one to be harmed by exorcism would be the demon itself. And he or she, as the case may be, would, of course, be violently opposed to it!"

"You mean I'm being influenced to oppose it."

"It's possible," he agreed.

I shook my head. "I don't know, Jimmy! I'm so confused. My thoughts feel like square pegs in round holes." That analogy seemed vaguely familiar. "I just wish everybody would leave me alone—the doctors, Tom, all of them! If I could just find out what Lucretia wants and do it, I'm sure I would be all right!"

"Amanda, please listen to me." He set his coffee cup on the bedside stand and leaned over to look me squarely in the eyes. "This is not something to play around with. It's high voltage! 'For we wrestle not against flesh and blood,' as Ephesians 6 says, 'but against principalities, against powers, against the rulers of the darkness. . . .' "

He walked over to the window, pulled back a curtain, and stood looking out over the foggy hospital grounds. From my bed, I could see scattered lights flicking on in the fog like the fuzzy white heads of dandelions. Suddenly, he let the curtain drop and turned back to me.

"Amanda, do you know the Lord?"

"Know him?" I stalled.

"Yes. Have you had a personal encounter with Jesus Christ, the Son of the living God?"

My stomach lurched, and a wave of nausea and dizziness swept over me. I swallowed hard. "We go to church," I hedged, avoiding his eyes.

He took me by the shoulders and forced me to look at him. "That's not what I asked you. Tom knows him. I assumed you did, too. That's why this whole thing puzzled me so. Now, I understand. You have had none of the protection God provides his own from evil spirits. Of course, God's own may unwittingly open themselves to attack, but you have been defenseless to it."

I pulled away from him. "And next you're going to tell me I have to make a choice, that only those who choose God have a right to his protection," I said, quoting Tom.

"That's right. Much as I'd like to—and I'm sure Tom even more so—no one can do it for you. *You* have to make the choice."

"I don't have to do anything but die and pay taxes, not necessarily in that order," I said flippantly.

"Jesus Christ took the punishment for your sins, Amanda," he said seriously. "You can reject his offer of salvation and go to hell if you want to. But don't kid yourself. By that very rejection, even if it is merely by indifference, you are making your choice."

I laughed shakily. "You sound just like Tom."

"I'll risk that," he said solemnly. "Have you ever read the book of Job? There's been a war going on between Satan and God ever since Satan got Adam and Eve to dig the first part of the chasm between God and man with their deliberate defiance of his will. God used his only Son to bridge that chasm, and all we have to do is walk that bridge, in faith, back to fellowship with him. But he won't push us across, Amanda. We either choose to join the army of God, or we automatically remain in Satan's ranks."

It all sounded so simple the way he and Tom saw it. For a moment, I wished I could accept it on their terms and be done with all the confusion. *If life is a war,* I thought, *he and Tom are well-trained soldiers, striding confidently through its battles. But I'm a*

*raw recruit, running first one way, then another,
confused and afraid.*

Suddenly, I was enveloped by a fury I didn't know
I possessed. "Where was your God when Lucretia
needed him so? Where was he when I was a lonely,
mixed-up child, when I would have given an arm and
a leg for a 'personal encounter' with anybody?"

A sadness came over his face, coupled with what
looked like a trace of fear. "Put aside your bitterness,
Amanda, and accept God's forgiveness and love."

"Forgiveness? He should ask *my* forgiveness! What
has he ever done for *me?* I've never done anything
against God. Why should he refuse to answer me?
Joel was a Christian, but he was shot down and de-
famed. Our children go hungry. . . ."

Sweat popped out across his forehead. "Amanda,
renounce this evil spirit," he begged. "Accept Jesus
Christ as your Savior and Lord!"

"I know your Jesus Christ," I sneered. The voice
was mine, yet the words were somebody else's lines
from a play gone awry. "He's never done anything but
torment me!"

"Torment you? Woman, he died for you!"

Then I began to laugh a weird, demonic laughter
that welled up from somewhere beyond my control.
He backed away, real fear in his eyes now. *The little
pious preachers are always the first to crack,* I
thought, having no idea what I meant by that. But
the laughter grew until it seemed to reverberate from
the walls.

"What on earth?" I hadn't known the nurse was in
the room. She ran out and was back almost instantly
with a needle in her hand. "You'll have to go, sir,"

she said firmly, inserting the needle in my arm. "You surely can see you are upsetting her!"

He hesitated, then turned toward the door. I watched him silently, eager to see the last of him. But he turned back, a look of determination on his face. "I'll be praying for you, that you will turn to the only One who can give you real peace. He won't force himself on you, but he loves you, Amanda, enough to have died for you. Remember that."

An overpowering sense of longing shook me, longing to be enfolded in the loving arms of a loving God, as I so often had longed for the arms of my father. I struggled to communicate this to Jimmy O'Brien, but I could not get the words past some blockage in my throat. I shook my head helplessly, tears spilling down my cheeks.

He took a step toward the bed. "Amanda."

I began to sob hysterically. "Just leave me alone!" I cried, not sure what I wanted, contradictory feelings at war within me.

"Please, sir," the nurse insisted, pushing him toward the door, "you must go!"

He went out, and the nurse followed, pulling the door behind her.

I'd never felt lonelier in my life. I opened my mouth to call him back, to ask him to help me find that peace both he and Tom possessed. But the sound that came from my throat—kept soft so as not to disturb the nurse—was gloating, triumphant laughter.

TWENTY-TWO

I opened my eyes and found Tom standing at the foot
of the bed. I glanced out the window. It was still dark
outside, except for the fuzzy dandelion lights and a
faint streak of a red dawn in the distance. The nurse's
needle had done its work. I must have slept for hours.

"Good morning, sweetheart," he said. "How are
you this morning?" He didn't move from the foot of
the bed or offer his usual good-morning kiss.

I rubbed my eyes. "A little disoriented. The nurse
gave me a shot last night that really packed a wallop!"

"Yes, I heard about it." His face wore lines I'd never
seen before. "I understand Jimmy O'Brien was here."

I put up a hand to rub my temple. "Was he? I
wasn't sure his visit wasn't just another of those crazy
dreams I've had all night."

"The nurse says she had to ask him to leave." His
eyes questioned me.

"Did she?" It was coming back to me now, but I

didn't want Tom's cross-examination. Suddenly, I remembered Tom's visit to Jimmy's office and the purpose behind it. "Did you find a priest?"

He nodded. "Father Werner. He says there isn't enough evidence that you are 'demon possessed' to convince the Church," he said sheepishly. I breathed a sigh of relief. "You have to give evidence of superior strength, clairvoyance, levitation, or speak or understand a foreign language you've never learned. I had to admit that all you did was believe you were living in the past. Father Werner says he feels sure the Church would not authorize an exorcism on those grounds. I think he believes you are schizo, in spite of the tests, and I think he wants no part of an exorcism. He cautioned me about the danger involved for the exorcist, as well as the possibility of making the patient worse. He gave me some books to read—"

"Tom," I broke in, "Dr. Platner admits there isn't much he can do to help me. Are you afraid to take me home? I feel perfectly all right now. Maybe Lucretia is satisfied with all the turmoil she has caused. Maybe she won't bother me again." *Or if she does,* I told myself silently, *I'll find out what she wants, do it, and get rid of her.*

"Well, I don't believe Dr. Platner is going to do you any good. That's for sure!" He stood studying me, as though trying to assess my condition for himself. "I want to talk with Jimmy O'Brien again."

I knew I had to get out of here before he saw Jimmy O'Brien! "Please, Tom," I begged, willing tears into my eyes. "I want to go home!"

"All right. We can always go somewhere else for help if you should. . . ." He hesitated. ". . . Be bothered again. And I still believe in the power of prayer. We'll go home, sweetheart."

I felt a surge of happiness. "Oh, Tom," I said impulsively, "I'm so sorry for all that's happened. I'll—"

He stopped my words with a kiss. Then, before he could kiss me again, I pushed him away.

"Unless you want to be guilty of wife-napping, or whatever taking a wife out of a hospital without permission is called, you'd better find Dr. Platner and get him to dismiss me."

He laughed and left the room obediently. I lay staring at the door as it closed behind him. I had pushed Tom away, not because I was worried about his seeing the doctor, but because his kiss had been repulsive to me. Could I ignore the telltale warning? Lucretia wasn't gone. I was sure of that. Yesterday, she had reacted to Jimmy O'Brien so strongly there was little I could do to control my words and actions. She had simply retreated again. That was all.

Once home, though, surely I could quickly accomplish whatever it was she wanted and be freed of her forever. This nightmare was no longer an amusing game. I was tired of the whole affair and more than a little afraid. Could I let her use me to accomplish her task and yet not lose my own identity entirely? I didn't know. I only knew staying in the hospital would not accomplish anything.

Dr. Platner wouldn't release me immediately. He was awaiting the results of more tests, he said. But all the tests proved negative; so that afternoon, at Tom's insistence, he let me go. Reluctantly, it seemed.

Tom whistled an off-key tune most of the way home, and I sat watching the dreary scenery go by, remem-

bering snatches from that night when he had taken
me on this journey in reverse.

As we got out of the car in our driveway, Black
Night left the front stoop, barking excitedly, and ran
to meet us. He stopped uncertainly at the end of the
walk and began to whimper, his tail between his legs.
He crept over to his doghouse, crawled inside, and
could not be coaxed out by either of us.

"You've been away several days. He'll have to get
used to you again," Tom apologized for him.

"Of course," I agreed quickly, doubting that was
the reason for the dog's behavior.

Inside, I wandered through the rooms, touching a
piece of furniture here, a vase or whatnot there. Out
of curiosity, I tried the gun cabinet and found it
locked. The key wasn't in the vase on the mantel,
either. I smiled. In Tom's position, I supposed I would
have taken the same precautions.

I insisted on fixing supper, and Tom sat at the
kitchen table talking as I broiled pork chops and
tossed a salad. "I'm glad you're home, sweetheart,"
he said. "You wouldn't believe how much I've missed
you! The bachelor's life is not for me!"

I sidestepped his reaching arms, pretending to
check on the pork chops. I still felt reluctant to let
him touch me, and I again sensed that chill of warning. Never, in all our married life before we'd moved
here, had I wanted to evade Tom's touch. I had trea-
sured that warm, safe feeling of his arms around me,
of cradling my head in the hollow of his shoulder. *I
just need time,* I told myself, pushing the warning
aside.

Tom seemed to sense my withdrawal. During our

meal, he made small talk, and afterward, as we watched a light comedy on television, he sat alone in his big chair. Not once did he motion for me to come sit scrunched beside him. At bedtime, he kissed me lightly, turned on his side, and soon was breathing deeply and evenly.

At least he trusts me not to shoot him in his sleep, I thought. But then, he had the gun locked up.

I tossed around, dozed a little, and woke again. Finally, to keep from disturbing Tom with my restlessness, I got up and went into the living room. The clock on the mantel said 2:00. I ran my fingers over the mantel. *It's amazing,* I thought, *how much dust and disorder can accumulate in three day's time in a practically empty house.*

That reminded me of Tom's reading about the evil spirit who had inhabited the empty house. Had my 'empty' soul been an invitation to Lucretia's wandering spirit, as Tom had suggested? Through the years, I had carefully built my defenses, keeping my inner self neat and tidy and uncluttered with anything that might make me vulnerable. Then I had met Tom, my defenses had crumbled, and I had let his love fill the empty spaces in my soul. I had thought this was enough until I had found that letter and had felt so utterly deserted.

Could something greater than human love fill those empty spaces so that nothing or nobody could make me feel alone again in that same desolate way? Certainly Tom and Jimmy O'Brien had something that I didn't.

Restlessly, I wandered through the house until my eyes fell on the book I had discarded the other night after I'd read about the woman possessed by the young girl who wanted vengeance. I picked it up and carried it to the kitchen where I fixed a cup of hot tea and sat down to read.

Many of our modern-day assassins, the book claimed, were possessed. Both Lee Harvey Oswald and Sirhan Sirhan had been involved with spiritualist cults, it said, and both claimed some mysterious "they" had told them to kill the Kennedy brothers. Oswald feared what he called "the devilmen," and Sirhan had scrawled a satanic motto in crayon near his victim.

President Garfield's killer, the book went on, had claimed "the Lordy," whom he sometimes identified as Satan and sometimes as God, had ordered him to shoot the President. The book went on for several pages telling of one murderer after another who had claimed to have been under the control of something outside himself when he committed the crime. One of them repeatedly had expressed the wish that he could have met Jesus, who could cast out demons.

Were the people of the Middle Ages with their belief in demon or spirit possession more right than we had dreamed? I wondered as I laid the book down and went back into the bedroom. Had the skepticism and hard-nosed God-is-dead-do-your-own-thing philosophy of so many of us moderns produced exactly the unprotected, susceptible state of soul the invading spirits needed to accomplish their aims?

I've definitely been influenced by something ever since I first saw that gray house, I thought as I crawled back into bed beside Tom. *But demon posses-*

sion is so archaic! I preferred to believe in an innocent, restless spirit like Lucretia.

Sometime later, I vaguely heard Tom's voice. Then
he shook me gently. "I'm going in to the office for
a while, sweetheart, but I'll be back before you need
to get up. OK?"

I mumbled something, turned over, and was sleeping soundly before he left the house, totally unaware
of how vulnerable his leaving made me.

TWENTY-THREE

I awoke to the sound of rain with the conviction that it had rained steadily all night. I could hear the roaring of the creek and knew it was running fast and out of its banks.

My head throbbed dully. My thoughts seemed crammed inside like a swollen drawer in a wooden dresser. The clock in the parlor struck the hour, and with its striking I felt a sinking sensation in my stomach, a deepening sense of impending disaster.

Ten o'clock was later than I usually awoke, and I rolled quickly out of bed, the creaking of the headboard lost in the roaring outside. . . .

. . . *I pulled aside the curtain to look out.* I'm not going to send the children to school in this weather.

The water was swirling angrily not twenty feet from our front door. The white foam that dotted the coffee-colored water reminded me of the times I unknowingly had poured sour cream into my coffee and had watched it float to the top, knowing I would have to pour out the whole cupful and start over with fresh cream, or if there was none, drink it black.

I heard a ringing sound and held my hands to my ears to shut it out of my aching head. Finally it stopped, and I turned back to the white-flecked waters outside. But why was I standing here dwelling on cream in coffee while the muddy water reached hungrily for the house? I would have to pack what we could carry, and the children and I would have to climb the hill behind the house to the Hawkins' place on the other side. We were cut off from the Adams' place by the rapidly rising water.

"I'm not going to Dora Hawkins!" I said aloud. "We'll just pass through their place and go on up the road somewhere. . . ." But, all at once, it seemed too much. I sank down on the bed, exhausted with my thoughts of one more battle for survival. The struggle to climb the thickly-overgrown hillside in the rain, half-carrying Susannah; the thought of losing the house and all we owned in the flood; searching for a place to stay temporarily, if not permanently.

If only I could lie down and go to sleep and never wake up.

"Ma!" Harrison's voice broke into my thoughts. I supposed he had seen the water. I pushed my weary bones up from the featherbed. I had to go on for the children.

"Ma! Ma! The water!" Susannah screamed. I could hear her whimperings and Harrison's tremulous voice as he tried to comfort her.

"It's all right, children!" I called. But would anything ever be all right for us again? *I wondered*

hopelessly as I dressed. Oh, we could, by a great effort, cross the hill and find shelter. The water would have to take the house before it could cover our escape route out back, and I judged that we had at least an hour or more before that would happen, if it ever would. The water had been known to drop suddenly and be back within its banks before we realized it.

But was escape worth the effort? Was life—this empty, plodding, meaningless existence—worth the effort?

I dressed Susannah and ordered the boys into boots and sturdy clothing. I didn't know how long the idea must have lain at the back of my mind, but as I fixed the children biscuits made with water and the last of the flour, it began to grow. The more I thought about it, the more simple and right it seemed. There's nothing to keep us here, and somewhere Joel is waiting. . . .

I jumped at the first knock on the front door, surprised that anyone would be out in this weather and with the flood at our door. I had a strange feeling that somehow that knocking did not belong. But perhaps Pa Adams had sent a boat to get us out. I listened, with the bread pan in my hand, knowing with certainty that even with easy rescue possibly just outside the door, I had no desire to be saved.

The knocking began again, but I ignored it. Maybe they would go away.

"Ma!" It was Harrison, and I knew he would answer if I didn't. Anyway, whoever was outside would have heard his voice and would know we were here.

I shook my aching head to clear it. Everything

seemed all wrong, as though this were a play I had rehearsed and now was being played with all the wrong cues.

I opened the door. "Tarrellton! What are you doing out in this?" But I should have known he wouldn't stay inside with a flood going on outside.

Fear flickered in his dark eyes. I supposed he was afraid I was going to punish him. Pity and love welled up in me. I had been so cross, so worried lately. I knew it had been extra hard on the children. I smiled at him. "Come on in, honey. Come in before you catch your death of cold!" Then I almost laughed. Where we were going none of us would ever be sick or cold or hungry again.

"Come on in," I repeated, for he simply stared at me. Then he shook his head, slowly but firmly, his solemn gaze never leaving mine.

"No, ma'am," he said. "I better not. I just told the minister I'd. . . ."

I had no time for his insolence. I reached for his arm to pull him inside. He resisted me with all his strength, and he was strong for his size. Rather than dragging him into the hallway, I found myself out in the rain. He was struggling frantically, and in his panic was heading straight for the water, dragging me along with him.

Why not? I thought suddenly. I wasn't sure I would have the courage to wade deliberately into that swirling water and take the children with me. But Tarrellton was taking me. It would be easier this way.

Icy tongues of the water licked at my ankles.

"Ma!" I heard Harrison scream. "Wait, Ma! Don't leave us!"

We couldn't go without the others! I couldn't leave them here without me! Neither could I let Tarrellton go into the flood alone. I half turned toward the house and saw them standing in the doorway, Susannah crying and clutching at Harrison's sleeve. I saw him reach for her hand, and I hoped desperately for them to follow us, as they had before.

"We're going this way, children!" I shouted, trying to make them hear above the roaring of the flood. They were running toward us, I saw in relief. But Tarrellton's struggles had increased. "Don't worry, darling," I shouted. "It soon will be over and we will be with your papa!"

"No! No! You killed him! You know you did!" he screamed. "You pushed him! I saw you!" His eyes were glazed with fear. He made a desperate lunge and tore himself from my grasp.

It hadn't been this difficult before, once the agonizing decision had been made. Tarrellton had struggled some, but we simply had walked into the water and had been swept along with the current. I had caught one brief, heartbreaking glance of the other two as they had been carried away from us. Soon all our bodies had ridden effortlessly and uncaringly over the bruising rocks of the creek bed.

Everything was all wrong this time. Tarrellton was gone, and somehow I was glad. I had the feeling that I had nearly repeated a terrible mistake. Before, death had not brought me peace. It had separated me from the children, and I never had found Joel.

I was down in the creek bed now, the muddy water swirling deeper around me. . . .

. . . Looking down in surprise, I saw that the creek

lay green and placid where I stood beneath the bridge in the deepest pool, which came just a little above my waist.

Shivering, I waded onto the rocks. It hadn't rained yet at all, though the sky looked as though there was going to be a deluge. The rocks at the water's edge were dry in the thin autumn sunlight that filtered through the black clouds. There was no water at all in the meadow behind me. Above the bridge, the water babbled contentedly over the rocks. Below the bridge, it was still dim and gloomy. If the overhanging elms were cut, would the sunlight ever warm and light that dreary spot . . . ?

I shivered as the memory of Lucretia's suicide played on the surface of my mind. Hurriedly, I returned to the house, stripped off my dripping clothes, and ran a tub of hot water. By the time I had bathed, dressed, and fixed myself a cup of hot chocolate, my teeth had stopped chattering, but my head still hurt terribly, and my mind felt like a raging torrent.

I went into the living room and turned on the TV, more for company than for the stupid soap opera that filled the screen. I hated soap operas. *Anyway, Lucretia's story is so much more absorbing,* I thought as I reached mechanically for a skein of the blue yarn and the knitting needles I had left on the lamp table beside my chair.

She had killed herself and the children. Mr. Rob had been wrong. And the good people of the church had buried her where they had refused to bury innocent Joel. *Had this ironic justice pleased her or angered her?* I wondered. Obviously the latter, for she felt passionate hatred for that church and its people.

I was glad, though, that she had shown me this last scene of her death. Now the story was ended. She had shown me the whole thing. What more could there be? She would leave me alone now.

Suddenly, as frightened as I had ever been in my life, I threw the yarn and the needles into a tangled pile on the floor and ran from the room. I, who could not knit, had counted expertly through a whole row of perfectly knitted stitches! Lucretia was with me still, and I knew I had none of Dr. Platner's confidence in my ability to control her.

I ran to the phone and dialed Tom's number, not really wanting him, but unwilling to be alone. I listened with a sinking heart to the uninterrupted ringing until, at last, I broke the connection.

In desperation, I went into the bathroom, grabbed a bottle of pain pills left over from Tom's bout with an infected tooth last winter, and with shaking hands poured two capsules into my palm. I gulped them down with water, forgetting Dr. Platner's theory about drugs and possession. My only thought was to sleep until Tom came home and I would be safe. But would I? Would I ever be safe again?

What more could she want of me? "What do you want?" I cried aloud. "Show me what it is you want, and I'll do it!" I sank back on the bed, exhausted, but somehow free of struggle. *The capsules,* I thought *gratefully as a numbness spread over me and I sank into sleep. . . .*

TWENTY-FOUR

. . . The wind was howling around the house and hurling itself against the windowpanes.

I sat up groggily. I had to do something. What was it? I massaged my throbbing temples. My mind seemed an echo of the howling confusion outside.

The house was dark and gloomy with the overcast day. I would have to light a lamp to see, even though it surely was just late afternoon.

Suddenly the plan, as fitting and beautiful as when I had first conceived it, clicked back into my mind. Today is Wednesday, and everything I need is there, I thought as I hurriedly tucked my hair into a bun at the nape of my neck. I had to get there before anyone came. I grabbed a wrap from the hall closet and went outside.

The wind was whipping the bare trees on the hill-

sides into a savage dance and flinging dust from the road into the air. It wrapped my skirts around my legs and snatched at the pins in my hair. A solid sheet of gun-metal sky had shut down over the valley like a lid on a seething kettle.

When the rain starts, it will come down like it's pouring out of buckets! *I thought. But I hadn't waited all this time to have my purpose defeated by the weather. I couldn't count on another opportunity like this one. I pushed myself to a faster pace, holding my aching side. I clutched my shawl around me and leaned into the wind, taking four steps to gain three.* . . .

I had no idea how long it took me to reach the church, but the tall gravestones finally came into view. I was as tired as if I'd done a winter's washing and made soap the same day. But it seemed I was early enough. No horses and buggies or carts stood in the churchyard.

I ran to the door, pressed the latch, and shoved against it. The hinges squeaked in protest, but the door swung open. I had to struggle against the wind to shut it again. Exhausted, I sank down on one of the back pews to catch my breath. I didn't want to complete my task yet, anyway. I wanted the people inside, all snug and content in their pews, piously holding prayer meeting when it happened.

Still, it would be best to have everything ready. I went to the closet at the front of the building and rummaged for the jug of kerosene I knew was kept there for filling the lamps and kindling fires in the wood stove. When I lifted it out, I pulled out the corncob stopper, but the lack of weight had already told me it was empty. Why hadn't I thought of that?

Frantically, I turned to the lamps and found that each of their bowls was nearly full. I grabbed them one by one, removed their chimneys, unscrewed their caps, and poured their contents into the jug. I replaced the caps and chimneys on the empty bowls and placed the lamps back on their stands. Then I picked up the jug and a handful of matches from the tin box on one stand and went back to the door. I had to get outside before the congregation began to arrive.

As I eased open the door, the wind snatched it from my hands and sent it crashing back against the wall. I threw a hurried glance outside and saw no one was there. Inside the door, I tilted the jug, sprinkling the dry wooden floor with about half of the kerosene.

It was a perfect day, if only the rain held off. The church was old and dry and, once alight, with the help of the wind, would burn like tinder!

Chuckling to myself, I pulled the door shut and hurried around behind the church to hide in the woodshed. It had only three sides, with the open side toward the church, but I would not be seen here unless they decided to build a fire and someone came for wood. That was unlikely, for Silas Hawkins rarely agreed to have a fire built unless it was so cold inside that a body's nose and feet were like lumps of ice before the minister started his sermon.

Just to be safe, though, I wedged myself behind a rick of cedar logs, inhaling the pungent, spicy odor as I waited. My limbs were getting cramped. I was thinking of leaving my hiding place to stretch them when I heard the first buggy pull into the churchyard.

Soon the yard was busy with wheels and the stamping and snorting of horses. Footsteps and indistinguishable voices were nearing the building. I couldn't hear the hinges of the door or any comments about the scent of kerosene. The voices were muffled now, I supposed they had gone inside and shut the door.

I waited quietly, the cramp of my limbs forgotten in anticipation. When I heard no more sounds of arrival, I crept out of hiding and around to the front of the church. It was nearly dark now, but apparently someone, aware of the jug's depletion, had brought some kerosene to refill the lamps. The high windows threw a faint yellow glow over the gravestones as the first notes of a hymn rose inside.

I had heard those sounds so many times. Even if no one had been inside, I could hear it all in memory, exactly as I was hearing it now. I stood at the corner of the building picking out Sophie Miller's tremulous soprano, William Smith's rumbling bass, the nasal whang of Dora Hawkins. They all were here! I stepped onto the front stoop with a feeling of glee.

I splashed the remaining kerosene over the wooden door and threshold, fumbled for a match, and struck it against the door frame. The wind blew it out. I struck another, my hands shaking with fear that someone would smell the added kerosene and come to investigate.

Shielding the flickering match with my hands and my shawl, I held it to the soaked wood. The flame reached for the kerosene and crackled hungrily up the door. I struck two more matches and lit other spots. The doorway was a sheet of licking flames. I backed away from their greedy tongues, tightly wrapping my shawl against the wind.

I knew I should go, but I wanted so much to stand in the churchyard where they had stood that day and self-righteously denied Joel a Christian burial in their precious sanctified ground. I wanted to hear the cries of fear and pain that would come from inside the church as the good hypocrites got a foretaste of hell.

It was strange that they hadn't cried out already, for the flames were reaching beyond the doorway, greedily consuming the dry wood around it. Surely they could hear that eager crackling and see the flickering light! But perhaps they were too piously wrapped up in their singing.

Footsteps plopped in the dry dust of the road! I turned quickly, peering through the deepening dusk, but I could see no one. Then a small figure ran toward me from out of the twilight. He was shouting, but I couldn't distinguish the words over the roaring of the wind and the flames.

He stopped just inside the fence, staring at the fire that now covered the whole front of the church. Then he ran insanely toward it, veering off at the last moment to one side where a gravestone stood alone beside the building. He stood there a moment, looking from the stone to the flames and back again. He turned back toward me, the flames clearly outlining the hatred in his face. It cut through me with a searing pain. I took a step toward him.

"You don't understand . . . ," I began.

"Go to hell where you belong!" he shouted. "Leave us alone!" He was crying now. I could see the glistening of tears on his cheeks and in his dark eyes. He dashed them away angrily with one hand and ran around the building.

I waited uncertainly. I hadn't thought about the children until now.

He was back with a bucket of water which he threw at the flames. They crackled hungrily, as though the water merely whetted their appetite. He disappeared around the church again.

Thunder rumbled in the distance and lightning flashed behind the church. I stood praying an unholy prayer to whatever might be listening that the rain would come too late.

He returned with another bucket of water and splashed it on the flames nearest the stone. Then, in frustration and futility, he threw the bucket at them, too. Illuminated by the flames, he sobbed aloud and cursed me as I laughed.

I wasn't laughing at him. I wanted to tell him that. But I couldn't stop. It felt so good to see the church burn. I rejoiced in it.

No one inside was going to scream, I guessed. Perhaps they had all been overcome by smoke. But they were in there all right! That was what mattered.

A roaring came in my ears above that of the fire and the wind. A door slammed, then another, and I heard voices shouting. I turned to run, but the path was blocked by two black shapes. I dodged to one side, but one of them reached out and grabbed me by the wrist. I tried to pull away and I still couldn't stop laughing.

"Amanda, stop it!" shouted the blond one I had seen before. He was shaking me. I laughed in his hateful face.

My head jerked back. The gray one had slapped me. I stopped laughing to glare at him, and his gray eyes bored into mine as though seeking something beyond them.

"Amanda," he said with authority, "this is Dr. Platner. Listen to me! You must take control!"

"In the name of Jesus Christ, leave her alone!" the other one ranted.

No! I thought. Never! I laughed in mockery.

"Amanda, help me!" the blond one begged. "Fight her! Sweetheart, I love you!" He stopped uncertainly, then determination hardened his features. "I won't let you go!" he vowed. "You must choose between this evil spirit and God!"

I struggled with him, trying to escape his eyes, his words.

"Amanda, God loves you!" He panted as he fought to hold me. " 'For God so loved the world,' " he quoted loudly, " 'that he gave his only begotten Son, that whosoever believeth in him should not perish, but have everlasting—' "

"No! Leave me alone—" I tried to tear myself from his grasp, but he held me, his voice relentless and hellish amid the crackling glow of the fire, quoting verse after verse.

" 'He that believeth on him is not condemned: but he that believeth not is condemned already. . . .' "

I tried to cover my ears with my hands, but he held them against my sides, and I had to listen to the hateful words.

A red-haired man ran up the walk, took in the scene, and joined him.

" 'Before anything else existed, there was Christ, with God. He has always been alive and is himself God. He created everything there is. . . .' "

Then his voice took on a new energy. " '. . . Eternal life is in him, and this life gives light to all mankind. His life is the light that shines through the darkness—and the darkness can never extinguish it.' "

My head was a crescendo of pain.

"In the name of the Father, the Son, and the Holy Spirit, I command you to leave her!" the red-haired one demanded.

"Amanda, ask God to help you!" the blond one cried.

I heard a crackling sound and whirled around. The empty bell tower was falling. A mighty roar went up from the fire as the roof collapsed in a geyser of sparks.

With one anguished cry, the boy flung himself across the gravestone just before the flaming tower hit it.

"God help me!" I screamed, the words wrenched from the depths of my being. "In the name of Jesus Christ, help me!" I ran toward him, stumbled, and fell to my knees as an agony of despair exploded in my head. In the heat and light of the flames, I felt the beginning of the cold darkness. . . .

. . . I was up and running again, praying and crying as I ran. "Oh, Chad, Chad!" I sobbed as I clawed barehanded at the burning wood. The tower was too heavy. I couldn't lift it!

Jimmy O'Brien pulled me away and took my place.

CHAPTER TWENTY-FOUR

Others were throwing water on the burning tower, prying it up off the stone.

Chad lay in a small crumpled heap across the top of the grave. There was the acrid scent of burned flesh, but it was from my hands. The fire had not reached Chad because the tower had fallen in a lean-to fashion across the stone. Chad, after he had been struck, had slid beneath it into the protected angle between it and the stone. Chad had thrown himself under the falling tower to protect his father's grave, as Tarrellton Palmer had thrown himself under the tree to save his son.

I knelt beside him, smoothing back the rumpled, thick dark hair from the ugly bruise on his forehead. "Your guilt is expiated now, Chad," I whispered, "but O God! How will I ever expiate mine?"

Dr. Platner knelt beside me. He raised one of Chad's eyelids and let it drop, laid his ear against the boy's chest, then reached for his wrist.

"He's dead," I said hopelessly.

The doctor shook his head. "There's a very faint pulse."

"Don't lie to me, doctor! Chad's dead! I killed him!"

Tom lifted me to my feet, and I rested my head against his chest, whimpering. His arms closed around me. "We've got to get those burns treated, sweetheart," he said gently. But the animal sounds coming from my throat were not for the burns on my hands and arms. They were the only way I could express the unutterable grief I felt.

An ambulance screamed to a stop in the parking lot, and I watched them lift Chad to a stretcher and hurry him away. My mind was a black hole of sorrow.

"It was Lucretia who set the fire," Dr. Platner murmured as he examined my hands, "not you, Amanda. You must remember that!"

Yes, I thought gratefully, *I must remember that.* She had had reason to hate the people of that church. Whatever she had done, her grief for Joel had been deep and real. All she had done later was the result of madness brought on by Joel's unfair death and the unsympathetic attitude of the people. And now they all were dead inside.

A new horror swept over me. Lucretia had no right to murder anybody, but least of all the people in this church tonight. They had done nothing to her. They hadn't been born until long after she had killed herself and her children! Could it be that Tom and Jimmy O'Brien had been right all along? Had none of it been Lucretia, but some clever demon who used Lucretia's tragic story to gain my sympathy, to destroy me and this church and its people?

"Tom," I whimpered, "the people in the church. . . . Do you know how many . . . ?"

"No one was in it, thank God!" he answered.

"A joint community Thanksgiving service was held at the high school tonight," Jimmy O'Brien added gratefully.

I sagged against Tom in relief. I hadn't burned up a whole church full of people after all! But Dr. Platner had been wrong. My moral scruples had not been able to control Lucretia or the demonic entity that had led me to set that fire. If people had been inside, their charred bones would be lying among the ashes of the building.

The dozen or so people who had gathered in the

churchyard merely watched the fire and speculated on its origin. They hadn't even tried to fight it. It had burned too fiercely. Now all that remained were a few isolated flames and sparks that rose up with each fresh gust of wind.

"Bring her straight to the clinic and I'll dress those burns," Dr. Platner was telling Tom. "Otherwise, I think she'll be all right now."

"She's gone," I said positively.

"Not 'she,' Amanda, 'it,' " Tom corrected.

I nodded. "It left me suddenly when I wanted so badly to reach Chad. Before then, I struggled to say the words you asked me to say, to reject it, but it was stronger than I. Only at that moment when Chad was struck down was I able to force the words past its will."

Oh, Chad! I thought, plunging back into that black, bottomless sorrow.

Tom held me closer to stop my trembling. "Let's go, sweetheart," he said. "Those hands have to be treated."

I obediently matched my steps to his, but my hands weren't bothering me that much. Their burning was the only way I seemed able to hurt for Chad. I knew how Lucretia must have felt when her grief had been "too deep for tears." How she must have suffered!

A shiver of fear slid down my spine. *God, don't let her . . . it come back!* I begged silently.

As Dr. Platner, Tom, and I drove away from the churchyard, I looked back at Lucretia's gravestone, half afraid I would see her standing there. Then I knew as surely as if the real Lucretia had put the thought in my mind that I had to do one more thing.

TWENTY-FIVE

From the edge of the woods, I looked back from my place directly behind the long cedar coffin and saw the small procession spread out down the hill behind the house.

There were the minister and the three elders from the church. What a time I'd had convincing them this was the right thing to do! But they came along with their deacons and the other men who were serving as pallbearers.

Behind the elders and the old man and his young friend, just rounding the corner of the house, came the sled with its regal stone passenger riding easily, if ignominiously, on its side.

I turned and followed the coffin bearers into the dimness under the thick trees. " 'The woods are lovely, dark and deep . . . ,' " I quoted softly. They *were* lovely, deep and mysterious, with only dappled patches of filtered sunlight to prove it was early afternoon.

Then, thinking that the next line of Frost's poem was even more appropriate, I whispered it also. " '. . . But I have promises to keep. . . .' " I felt a kind of peace that, at last, an old wrong was being righted.

The bearers had stopped and were placing their heavy burdens over their final resting places. The tractor pulling the sled also had stopped, and neither birds' song nor squirrels' chatter invaded the hushed reverence. Even the wind and the cedars' whispery branches were still.

Jimmy O'Brien opened his Bible and began to read, his vibrant voice seeming out of place in the quiet woods. " 'Peace I leave with you, my peace I give unto you: not as the world giveth, give I unto you. Let not your heart be troubled, neither let it be afraid. . . .' "

My gaze wandered over the small group—the men in their topcoats hunched against the early December chill, the girl with red knees showing between her short skirt and high boots. And against the oak with the embedded stone, I could almost see a young boy, seemingly impervious to the weather in a shrunken sweater and thin jeans. Quickly, I turned my thoughts back to the minister's words.

They were more for the living than the dead, but perhaps that was as it should be. It was too late to help the dead. I knew that now. Lucretia, like all of us, had been given one lifetime to find her way to God. If she had not, I didn't believe there was a second chance. Of course, I couldn't say what God would or would not do. I only knew that I could do nothing about it.

Even this moving of the gravestone was little more than a gesture, for nothing but soil had remained where the bodies had lain. The diggers had carefully placed the soil from the four graves in four new cedar boxes. These now rested over freshly-dug graves in a square beside the stone tree stump with its squirrel and its inscription from John 5:24. If only Lucretia had believed what she had had written on that stone, she, too, might have "passed from death unto life" and found, not only Joel, but peace.

" 'And the peace of God, which passeth all understanding, shall keep your hearts and minds through Christ Jesus.' " The minister's benediction, which he identified as being from Philippians 4:7, echoed my thoughts. Gratefully, I recalled the cleansing tide of absolution that had washed over me as I had stepped out onto that cross-shaped bridge and, before the congregation I had most wronged, had publicly confessed my desire to be on God's side.

I felt that God had granted me forgiveness for my indifference, for my transgressions, and, most of all, for Chad. But would I ever be able to forgive myself? Chad would always be there to flash painfully across my memory with teasing dark eyes and elusive charm, to haunt me as Lucretia never had.

The men were lowering the four boxes on ropes into the open graves—one long and three smaller ones—and those who had been hired for digging began to fill them.

A breeze had sprung up, and Mr. Rob's young clerk huddled inside her fake fur jacket, her nose turning red in spite of her makeup. "Do you think she's at rest now, Mrs. Farris?" she almost whispered, glancing nervously at the graves.

"I hope so," I answered. "I'm not sure where Lucretia Adams is, but I am now convinced that it wasn't that poor lady who caused my problems." I turned to Mr. Rob. "Why did whatever it was wait all these years for me?"

" 'There is a kind of sympathy in souls that fits them for each other—,' " Mr. Rob began.

"Can you honestly imagine any self-respecting ghost wanting to come back as Callie Palmer or old Mrs. Tupts?" Daren Blake broke in, winking at Janie, who giggled.

I smiled faintly in response to Daren's grin. I really didn't think it was funny. Mr. Rob's quote seemed much more appropriate. I *had* felt such sympathy for Lucretia. Even when the church officers had argued that it would be less trouble and less expensive to move Joel to the churchyard, I had known she would not have wanted it that way. And I was sure Chad, her only living relative, would rather she was as far from his dad as possible.

Oh, Chad! I thought for surely the thousandth time. *I'm so sorry! I wanted to do so much for you, and all I've done. . . .* But I turned my thoughts from that direction where only madness lay.

"Do you think you'll be bothered by . . . whatever it was again?" Janie whispered.

I shook my head. "I don't think so, Janie. Surely whatever it is will recognize that my 'empty house' has been filled by the Spirit of God. There's no room for it now."

"Oh," she said. "Well, thanks for inviting us to the . . . uh . . . funeral. It was. . . ." She stopped, obviously at a loss for words.

"Interesting," Daren finished for her. "What this

town has needed for a long time was a good, rousing funeral!" He laughed and turned to help Mr. Rob down the hill.

"You take care, little lady," Mr. Rob called over his shoulder. "And any time you have a chocolate cake going to waste, you know where to find me!"

I laughed. "I'll see you Monday morning, Mr. Rob. And thanks!"

It would take Tom and me a long time to repay the loan we had negotiated at the local bank to pay Chad's hospital bills, to move the graves, and to help rebuild the church. Tom was going back to his old law firm four days a week, and I was grateful for the job Mr. Roberts had offered me in the county court clerk's office. Helping to make restitution would make me feel better, although I could never give the congregation back its pre-Civil War building. And I could never make Chad well again.

One of the elders from the church was thanking Tom for our donation. "That plus the insurance should put us up a right comfortable little building. Meanwhile, we'll look forward to seeing you and your wife at our services at the YMCA," he said.

"Oh, Jimmy," I said as the minister stopped to say good-bye, "what will I do if Chad dies? I can't. . . ."

He reached out and clasped both my cold hands in his. "If that happens, we will face the jury together—you, Tom, Dr. Platner, and I—just as we did the judge. No one who knows the whole story blames you for what happened to Chad, Amanda, not even his mother."

"Callie Palmer has believed all along that Lucretia Adams killed her husband," I reminded him. "It isn't hard for her to believe she tried to kill Chad, too." Chad's mother had taken his injury rather well, except for one brief spell of faintness that first night at the hospital. Two men I hadn't seen before had helped her considerably. Afterward, she had left with one of them.

It wasn't Callie Palmer for whom I grieved. It wasn't even for the fact that, if Chad died, my five-year probation for "arson while temporarily insane" would be revoked and I would be tried for manslaughter. My grief was for Chad himself—all that impish charm and worldly-wise pessimism.

"I wouldn't get too attached to him if I was you," he had cautioned me about Black Night as he had romped with the dog in my backyard. If only I had heeded that advice about Chad himself!

"But, Jimmy, how do I stop blaming myself?" I blinked away the tears that flooded my eyes.

"Don't let a guilt trip for something over which you had no control cripple your soul, Amanda," he warned, "just when you've learned what it means to have a soul."

When I had made my last visit to the clinic on the judge's orders to continue "psychiatric treatment as long as deemed necessary," Dr. Platner had told me, "I believe you will be fine now, as long as you don't let guilt erode your mind."

I knew all the reasons I should not feel guilty. The evil force that had imitated Lucretia had set that fire, not I. Chad had thrown himself on his father's grave in a protective gesture born out of his own hardly understood guilt feelings. But I also knew all the reasons I was to blame. I had treated possession like a game, and I had found that, like the proverbial riding of a tiger, it was something one began much more easily than one stopped.

Jimmy squeezed both my hands. "Chad responded to my voice this morning by squeezing my hand just like this," he said. "The doctors are encouraged. But whatever happens, Amanda, he is safe in the hands of the Lord." His blue eyes showed clearly that he believed what he was telling me. Then suddenly, his eyes filled with tears. He wiped them away with the back of his hand. "I miss him, too," he admitted. "But just keep praying!" He turned and started down the hill.

"Let's go, sweetheart," Tom said, putting an arm around me. "They're almost finished here."

I looked over at the men maneuvering the stone into place in the midst of the four graves. A slight drifting movement, like a swirling of fog, caught my eye. Then I saw her standing between the stones, watching me out of dark, sorrowing eyes. Quickly, I closed my eyes. "In the name of Jesus Christ, my Savior and Lord, I renounce you, whatever you are!" I prayed quietly.

"Come on, sweetheart," Tom urged. "We can go home now and forget about Lucretia Adams."

Forget? I opened my eyes to stare at him in amazement. Didn't he understand, even yet, the sympathy that had lain between us? Even though I had no feeling for whatever had, apparently, used Lucretia's image and history to involve me in its evil schemes, I still felt deeply for the real Lucretia.

I let Tom turn me toward our house where we would soon spend Christmas together. *I'll make cedar wreaths for the graves,* I promised. *And in the summer, I'll bring black-eyed Susans.* It was all I could do for her now, all I ever should have done.

And for Chad? *Oh, Chad!* I thought, feeling again the sharp, black thrust of grief. *If you die, I'll never be able to do anything for you either, except ache endlessly and bring you poison ivy leaves in peanut butter jars.*

The thought was as hopeless and bitter as one of Lucretia's, and involuntarily I glanced back at the graves.

If anything had been there, it was gone now. Beside Lucretia's graceful white obelisk, Joel's stone proclaimed:

> *. . . He that heareth my word, and believeth*
> *on him that sent me, hath everlasting life,*
> *and shall not come into condemnation;*
> *but is passed from death unto life.*
> John 5:24

"Death unto life," I whispered, noticing the bare winter canes of the white rosebush in front of the stone.

The rose—its roots thrust deep into Lucretia's vanished time, its thorny stems a part of my own— bridged our two worlds and beyond. *In the spring, Lord willing, Chad and I will plant a slip of that white rose on Lucretia's grave. . . .*

Tom's arm around my shoulder turned me once again away from the graveyard. We stood looking down the wooded slope to the steep, overhanging roof of the gray house nestled in its peaceful valley. "A beautiful place!" Tom said softly. "I can hardly believe it's ours."

It really is ours now, I thought with a rush of gratitude. *Not a heritage, but a promise. And ours alone.*

I put my arm around Tom and we started down the hill toward the house, knowing in reality that safe, warm feeling of coming home.

Other Living Books Best-sellers

WHAT WIVES WISH THEIR HUSBANDS KNEW ABOUT WOMEN by James Dobson. The best-selling author of *DARE TO DISCIPLINE* and *THE STRONG-WILLED CHILD* brings us this vital book that speaks to the unique emotional needs and aspirations of today's woman. An immensely practical, interesting guide. 07-7896 $2.95.

HINDS' FEET ON HIGH PLACES by Hannah Hurnard. A classic allegory of a journey toward faith that has sold more than a million copies! 07-1429 $3.50.

MORE THAN A CARPENTER by Josh McDowell. A hard-hitting book for people who are skeptical about Jesus' deity, his resurrection, and his claims on their lives. 07-4552 $2.95.

LOOKING FOR LOVE IN ALL THE WRONG PLACES by Joe White. Using wisdom gained from many talks with young people, White steers teens in the right direction to find love and fulfillment in a personal relationship with God. 07-3825 $2.95.

ROCK by Bob Larson. A well-researched and penetrating look at today's rock music and rock performers, their lyrics, and their life-styles. 07-5686 $2.95.

GIVERS, TAKERS, AND OTHER KINDS OF LOVERS by Josh McDowell and Paul Lewis. This book bypasses vague generalities about love and sex and gets right to the basic questions: Whatever happened to sexual freedom? What's true love like? Do men respond differently than women? If you're looking for straight answers about God's plan for love and sexuality, this book was written for you. 07-1031 $2.50.

THE POSITIVE POWER OF JESUS CHRIST by Norman Vincent Peale. All his life the author has been leading men and women to Jesus Christ. In this book he tells of his boyhood encounters with Jesus and of his spiritual growth as he attended seminary and began his world-renowned ministry. 07-4914 $3.95.

MOUNTAINS OF SPICES by Hannah Hurnard. Here is an allegory comparing the nine spices mentioned in the Song of Solomon to the nine fruits of the Spirit. A story of the glory of surrender by the author of *HINDS' FEET ON HIGH PLACES.* 07-4611 $3.50.

NOW IS YOUR TIME TO WIN by Dave Dean. In this true-life story, Dean shares how he locked into seven principles that enabled him to bounce back from failure to success. Read about successful men and women—from sports and entertainment celebrities to the ordinary people next door—and discover how you too can bounce back from failure to success! 07-4727 $2.95.

HOW TO BE HAPPY THOUGH MARRIED by Tim LaHaye. One of America's most successful marriage counselors gives practical, proven advice for marital happiness. 07-1499 $2.95.

Other Living Books Best-sellers

LIFE IS TREMENDOUS! by Charlie "Tremendous" Jones. Believing that enthusiasm makes the difference, Jones shows how anyone can be happy, involved, relevant, productive, healthy, and secure in the midst of a high-pressure, commercialized society. 07-2184 $2.50.

THROUGH GATES OF SPLENDOR by Elisabeth Elliot. This unforgettable story of five men who braved the Auca Indians has become one of the most famous missionary books of all times. 07-7151 $3.50.

SONG OF ABRAHAM by Ellen Gunderson Traylor. A richly colorful novel that portrays a man of strength, will, and purpose, a man who remains unparalleled in history. Carefully researched and superbly told, this memorable account can be read both for enjoyment and information. 07-6071 $4.50.

400 WAYS TO SAY I LOVE YOU by Alice Chapin. Perhaps the flame of love has almost died in your marriage. Maybe you have a good marriage that just needs a little "spark." Here is a book especially for the woman who wants to rekindle the flame of romance in her marriage; who wants creative, practical, useful ideas to show the man in her life that she cares. 07-0919 $2.50.

MARY MAGDALENE by Ellen Gunderson Traylor. *Mary Magdalene* sweeps into the life of the renowned follower of Jesus, a woman whose sorrows rival her beauty. Interwoven with biblical narrative, this story promises hope and healing for wounded hearts. 07-4176 $3.95.

THE BEST CHRISTMAS PAGEANT EVER by Barbara Robinson. A delightfully wild and funny story about what happens to a Christmas program when the "Horrible Herdman" brothers and sisters are miscast in the roles of the biblical Christmas story characters. 07-0137 $2.50.

LORD, I KEEP RUNNING BACK TO YOU by Ruth Harms Calkin. In prayer-poems tinged with wonder, joy, humanness, and questioning, the author speaks for all of us who are groping and learning together what it means to be God's child. 07-3819 $2.95.

LORD, IT KEEPS HAPPENING . . . AND HAPPENING by Ruth Harms Calkin. The author continues her prayer-poem dialogue with God, sharing moments of reflection and insight, silence and worship, renewed hope and sustained joy. 07-3823 $2.95.

THE CHILD WITHIN by Mari Hanes. The author shares insights she gained from God's Word during her own pregnancy. 07-0219 $2.95.

JOHN, SON OF THUNDER by Ellen Gunderson Traylor. In this saga of adventure, romance, and discovery, travel with John—the disciple whom Jesus loved—down desert paths, through the courts of the Holy City, to the foot of the cross. Journey with him from his luxury as a privileged son of Israel to the bitter hardship of his exile on Patmos. 07-1903 $4.50.

Other Living Books Best-sellers

ROOM FOR ONE MORE by Nyla Booth and Ann Scott. Ann and Phil Scott, with two daughters of their own, found themselves adopting not one, but eventually fifteen needy children. A heartwarming true story. 07-5711 $3.50.

SUSANNA by Glen Williamson. Meet Susanna Wesley, the mother of John and Charles Wesley, a most unusual though lesser-known woman of Christian history. This stirring testimony will challenge Christians to establish a strong foundation of faith for their children. 07-6691 $3.50.

LORD, COULD YOU HURRY A LITTLE? by Ruth Harms Calkin. These prayer-poems from the heart of a godly woman trace the inner workings of the heart, following the rhythms of the day and the seasons of the year with expectation and love. 07-3816 $2.95.

BITTERSWEET LOVE by Betty R. Headapohl. In this touching romance, Trevor, a wealthy land developer, falls in love with Starr, a health food store owner. Then Starr's former fiancé reappears, and the sparks start to fly. 07-0181 $3.50.

HUNTED GUN by Bernard Palmer. Colorado rancher John Breck encounters an ambush, suspicious townspeople, and deceit spawned by gold fever in this fast-paced yet thoughtful western for adults. 07-1497 $3.50.

HER CONTRARY HEART by Lois T. Henderson. A fascinating historical romance revealing the inner turbulence of a young and spirited woman who questions the tenets of the strict Harmonist Society to which she belongs. 07-1401 $3.95.

SUCCESS: THE GLENN BLAND METHOD by Glenn Bland. The author shows how to set goals and make plans that really work. His ingredients of success include spiritual, financial, educational, and recreational balances. 07-6689 $3.50.

KAREN'S CHOICE by Janice Hermansen. College students Karen and Jon fall in love and are heading toward marriage when Karen discovers she is pregnant. Struggle with Karen and Jon through the choices they make and observe how they cope with the consequences and eventually find the forgiveness of Christ. 07-2027 $2.95.

LET ME BE A WOMAN by Elisabeth Elliot. In these days of conflicting demands and cultural pressures, what kind of woman do you wish to be? With profound and moving insights, this best-selling author presents her unique perspective of womanhood. 07-2162 $3.95.

RAISING CHILDREN by Linda Raney Wright. Twelve well-known Christian mothers give their views on parenthood, sharing insights and personal experiences from family life that will both amuse you and cause you to think. 07-5136 $2.95.

The books listed are available at your bookstore. If unavailable, send check with order to cover retail price plus $1.00 per book for postage and handling to:

Christian Book Service
Box 80
Wheaton, Illinois 60189

Prices and availability subject to change without notice. Allow 4–6 weeks for delivery.